I0586681

Tied
Down

TIED DOWN COPYRIGHT

Publisher © Chelle Bliss & Eden Butler
June 12th 2018
Editor: Silently Judging Your Grammar
Proofreaders: Julie Deaton
Cover Design: Lori Jackson
Formatting: Allusion Graphics

Tied Down

CHELLE BLISS
EDEN BUTLER

Chapter One
Kiel

The woman two rows ahead of me knew she was beautiful. She knew how to work what the good Lord gave her. She also knew I was watching.

"Would you like another whiskey, Mr. Kaino?" It was only the soft twang in the flight attendant's voice that got my attention off the curvy brunette sitting in first class.

"Please," I told her, not able to keep the wink from my eye. Couldn't keep from watching the woman's face as she leaned over my tray and topped off my drink. She smelled like peaches, all sweet and tantalizing.

The whiskey went down with a bite, something I found oddly comforting. Something that did little to keep the swirl of arousal from my gut when the leggy brunette a few rows ahead of me rubbed her ankle, thumb pressing down into the arch of her foot before she shifted a gaze over her shoulder, eyes lidded, fucking sexy and dark.

My brother Kane had schooled me about women. Especially women like this. But his opinions shifted to the old-school kind. He liked to play the protector. He liked to be straightforward, honest about what he wanted. But Kane was happily besotted back in Seattle with his love Kit Carlyle. And currently, the cable viewing audience and the rest of the country were taken by the PDA on their home improvement show.

Kane could have his woman and the happily ever after they were building together. Me? I liked to play. I liked the game, and I was fucking good at it.

I took in the look Legs gave me, watched the slip of her small tongue against her bottom lip. Spotted the tease of cleavage when she bent down, stretching to grab her shoe that had somehow ended up in the next row over. Accident? I'm sure, but deep down, I hoped she'd started the game—one I'd win. One that would end with me leaning back as that sexy woman rode me in the airport bathroom.

It would be a good way to welcome myself back to New York. Celebrate in a JFK stall. Maybe a service closet because no one was expecting me until the next morning anyway. I shot a smile at Legs, who was currently stretching, standing to the overhead compartment to retrieve something. Another move she made that told me she was good at game-playing herself. She wore a fitted skirt and a flowy blouse with a cinched waist. It made that glorious body look dangerous, and I was in the mood to be a little reckless. Legs looked around the cabin, shrugging to herself when no flight attendant approached, and pulled open the compartment, grabbing what looked like a small wallet.

Legs turned to face me, adjusting something in her seat that brought her body facing me. She moved her gaze from the blanket she pretended to fix, right to my face. I held that sharp gaze a full six seconds, examining the planes of her pretty face. The smooth, young skin, the pronounced angles of her chin, and the thin top lip dwarfed by a bottom lip that had no business being that full and that damn sexy. Green eyes, from what I could make of them and perfectly trimmed, arched brows. She was just this side of being too polished, too well put-together, but that only added to her appeal. I felt a deep-down craving to muss her perfect hair and smear her lipstick, all over my stomach and...

Legs stood straight, grabbing her small bag before she left her seat. Hips in a tempting sway as she walked toward me. I got an up-close look, and my suspicions were confirmed: fucking glorious, gorgeous, and *definitely* interested. No one looks at a perfect stranger the way she looked at me. Not unless they were attracted, and holy hell, did that look promise she was a shit-ton more than attracted.

Her gaze went primal, hungry. The way she let her eyes glide over my face, right down to my lap, told me all I needed to know. She was biding her time. Maybe waiting for me to make a move, speak just a little to encourage her. But I was good at the game, remember? You don't show your hand so soon after the game has started.

When she swept by my seat, close enough to reach out and touch my shoulder, I moved, leaning my seat back, smiling at the heat I felt from her stare as I closed my eyes. I caught her perfume as she moved by me —a fucking delicious scent that made me want to dive right between her thighs—and I licked my lips, wondering if she spotted the movement, hoping it frustrated her that I was playing distant.

The smell of her perfume disappeared, and I moved the smile off my face, making a mental note to thank my new boss Raquel for the shot at the crime beat in one of the most prestigious papers in the country—*and* the first-class ticket. I felt like a king, comfortable, smug at having caught the attention of such a gorgeous woman, but then one of the flight attendants went around the plane, asking for final requests, and I knew we'd be landing soon.

Since I got the job offer, there'd been an acute sense that something was off. Something that made me a little suspicious. I was a great writer. I was even better at researching and pressing leads for information, but I wasn't the best. Not just yet. So why did I land this gig? And in New York, of all places?

It was probably stupid to be paranoid. Likely even more asinine to listen to my big brother's warning before I left Seattle.

"Watch your back, Kiel. That family has a long reach."

He meant the Carellis. He meant the past.

Five years ago, Cara Carelli had jerked me into her criminal world with her mouth and hands, with her warm thighs and hotter pussy. She'd driven me away from who I was and any semblance of who I wanted to be. I'd loved her. I'd have done anything for her.

I'd been a punk kid just finishing up a journalism degree at NYU. She'd been the troubled source I ran into while trying to break a huge story. That story ended up with me getting the shit beat out of me and her brother and her father's goons laughing at me as I bled out on the pavement. She'd told the cops I was a stalker. She'd told her family she didn't know me at all. None of those things was true.

I knew Cara. I knew exactly where she lived and how she tasted.

It took years for me to get my head on right. It took a lot of liquor and days of listening to my brother tell me what I'd done wrong and how not to do it again.

Cara had lied, and when I'd left New York after graduation with my killer story a bust, my internship done, and my heart ripped to shreds, I promised myself I'd never go back.

And here I was. About to land in the one place I told myself I never wanted to be again.

What the hell was I doing?

"You know." I heard, moving my head to the side when that familiar perfume filled my sinuses again. "I have a two-hour layover."

"Is that so?" I slid my arm behind my head, blinking my eyes open to see Legs staring down at me. She nodded, pressing her lips together, looking hungry. The brunette rested an arm on the headrest of my seat, and I pulled on her wrist, examining her left hand just to have something to do. She let me take her fingers, press them against my palm. Her skin was soft, supple like her body, and her nails were long, shaped but neat. "I might be able to help you fill your time." I sat up when she pulled her hand away, pretending to be a little wary of me. Then when I turned toward her, resting on my elbow, she fought a smile. "I might be able to fill a few things."

A quick blush crept across her face. She didn't frown or seem at all put off by my innuendo. I got a noncommittal shrug for my effort before Legs returned to her seat, shooting one final glance my way before the captain came on the overhead speaker, informing everyone to return to their seats.

"Your glass, Mr. Kaino?" The flight attendant held out her hand, and I nodded, slamming back the contents of my whiskey, licking my lips clean before I handed over the glass, throwing the woman a wink for her trouble. But my head was still in the game and working out how to be smooth and subtle, just to see where Legs wanted to go.

Central Park was the first thing you spotted when you descended toward New York. It went on forever, miles and miles of lush green in the center of buildings that seemed to stretch and reach beyond anything you could see. There were skyscrapers and landmarks all clustered tightly together, and in the middle of all that, the massive park. Just the sight of it brought back picnics with Cara and the lies that spilled from her mouth.

Legs spared one final glance my way, eyebrows up in a silent question, and I grinned, moving my chin down to answer her. It was on, and I had every intention of starting my life in New York inside this beautiful, welcoming woman.

"Enjoy your stay," the flight attendant said, slipping something into my hand as I left the plane. I guessed what it was before I hit the jetway, fisting the wad of paper with a random phone number as I moved into the airport.

Legs was four feet in front of me, hips swaying, fluffing her hair as she moved toward baggage claim to grab her luggage. There was one small bag waiting for her. I didn't have anything but the duffle on my shoulder, but I waited, hanging back as she grabbed her suitcase, pretending to be more interested in my phone than the beautiful woman who slipped through the crowd, tossing a curious glance at me.

Kane had texted about my flight, and I winked at Legs, not watching the screen. I sent my brother a quick "just landed" text before I walked behind the woman, catching up to her as she headed toward a hallway sealed off with an "Employees Only" sign haphazardly taped to the wall. I focused on the slow tap of her heels and the roll of her suitcase wheels moving ahead of me and not the vacant hallway or abandoned cleaning equipment around us.

Legs disappeared through the last door on the left, and that gut instinct of worry returned.

The woman stood against an empty wall, hands tucked demurely behind her back as she waited for me. She'd already taken her shoes off and moved her bag to the side.

Two steps from her, I paused, securing her hand against my chest when she held up her palm. "How do you know about this place?"

Legs shrugged, and there was a playful smirk moving her top lip. "I know people."

"You don't know me," I told her, licking my lips when she curled her fingers around my collar.

"I'm about to."

A small release of sweet, bourbon-tinted breath and I grabbed Legs by the back of the neck, stumbling just a little when that full mouth dropped open and she offered me her tongue. She hummed against my mouth, seeming to get a thrill at how I held her, how tightly I fisted her skirt in between my fingers when she stepped closer.

"Shit...you taste so good," she told me, as though she were surprised. She didn't pause for long and gripped my hair, moving my face closer, pressing her whole body against mine. "Better than I thought you would."

Her hair was thick lush, and I twirled it between my fingers, using it to guide her head to the left as I licked a path along her neck. "You taste exactly like I thought you would. Sweet." I nibbled at the dip beneath her throat, then up to her ear. "Succulent." Teeth tugging on her lobe, I released the smallest growl. "Hot."

"Ah..."

Legs was a beautiful woman, and despite how my mother had raised me, despite what I knew was right and wrong, I was about to fuck her in an empty bathroom at the JFK airport. It made no sense to want this woman, but I did. She reminded me of...

"Antonia!" I heard, and the woman in my arms broke away from me, pushing me back against the wall like she wasn't supposed to be anywhere near me.

"I..."

Two oversized men stood in the center of the room, stoic and stern, but neither of them had called her name. The sound of clicking heels met us from behind those men, and they broke apart, moving aside, and the clicking got louder.

Cara stood in front of us, looking fierce. More beautiful than I'd ever seen her, but she paid no attention to me. She glared at Legs, her face tight with anger. "I told you to get him here," she said, taking two more steps that put her right in front of us. "I never said you could try to fuck my *husband*."

Tension moved between my shoulders at the sound of her voice, and that feeling I'd had all day burned inside my gut like a virus. Cara moved her head, gesturing for Legs to leave before she faced me. There was something cool and detached in her features, and just that look was warning enough. I should have bolted for the door.

Fucking hell, I should have listened to my brother's warning.

But I hadn't, and just then, Cara faced me, keeping her features stern and her eyes dull.

"Hi, Kiel," she said, reaching out a hand to adjust my tie. "Welcome home."

Chapter Two
Kiel

Two big assholes, not a neck between them, stood watching me. Maybe they wanted me to back up, because their sheer size was something that might make a regular guy get a little worried. I wasn't a regular guy. Don't let the tie or the NYU degree fool you. I could start—and finish—shit no matter the size of the asshole coming at me. My brother taught me to stand when you could and walk away when you couldn't. Two against one, all the exits blocked, I knew well enough to stand my ground.

Cara's goons were strangers. At least, their squat faces weren't familiar. Definitely wasn't her brother. I remembered the exact structure of her brother's features and the faces of every meathead her father employed. I'd seen those faces twisted up in fury as they screamed at me, threw threats and promises my way that still made my fists tighten when I thought of it. But the two men blocking my exit weren't familiar.

"They don't speak English," Cara explained when I shot a glare at those roughnecks, asking who they were with a twist of my chin in their direction. "I hired them."

"I don't care."

That stung her. At least, that's what I picked up on when she flinched at my reaction ten seconds after Legs, or I guess Antonia was her name, hurried out of the room. "I know things didn't end well with us," Cara tried, and I shook my head, disregarding her with a quick flip of the bird as I made like I would follow Legs's lead. But the meatheads blocked my path. Their expressions, all hapless and angry, told me they hadn't liked me flipping off their boss.

Outnumbered or not, I felt my anger swell high enough that I got in the mood for a scuffle. Cara always made me want to hit something. Just then, it was the assholes crowding me when I tried to walk away.

"You boys want shit to get messy?" I asked them, knowing I couldn't take them all on my own, but not caring about that fact. Instead, I loosened my tie, readying myself. "Not real happy about getting busted and bruised, but fuck it. I haven't had a good tussle in weeks."

I dropped my jacket, tossing it onto the duffle next to the wall, and popped my neck just before Cara took hold of my arm, turning me to face her. "Like I said, *chooch*. They don't speak English." Her olive complexion brightened, those high cheekbones accentuated by a deep pink color.

"Fine," I told her, pulling out of her reach. I didn't bother commenting on the insult she'd flung at me. It was a habit she hadn't gotten rid of, but she could call me a jackass all she wanted. That wouldn't stop me from leaving. "Tell them to get out of my way."

"I need to talk to you." She curled her arms tightly. Her toned bicep flexed before she took two steps back when I grabbed my duffle and jacket, stuffing my loose tie into my pocket. Her mouth was tight, as though it took her more composure than she had not to scream because I wasn't immediately falling at my knees in front of her. Those black eyes of hers widened, lashes blinking fast as she watched me. I hated that she was still so beautiful. Even with the frown breaking from her twitching mouth, those thick, pink lips smoothing together, and the shift of her attention from my face to the room around us, she still was fucking beautiful.

"We can't..." She waved a hand around the bathroom, nose curling as she spotted the empty urinals and stalls with no toilets inside them. "I'll take you to your hotel. We'll talk there."

One thing I learned about Cara Carelli in the brief months we'd been married: you don't argue. Not about the small shit anyway. You gave her what she wanted and then got the hell away from her. She'd come back and want something else, but it was that first request that meant the most to her.

She wanted the upper hand.

She wanted the game to start in her favor.

She wanted you to know she could get anything she wanted from you, no matter how stupid the request.

This would be the only one I'd give her.

Her gaze was like a lick of fire as she watched me shrug on my jacket. Each movement she seemed to memorize, but I didn't watch her, not when I straightened my collar or fastened the open buttons on my shirt. That stare was something I remembered. It was something that burned like a snake bite pushing venom into my veins. It was something you had to ignore, or it would set your entire body ablaze. I gave up loving that burn a long time ago, but the scars would likely never heal.

I didn't bother acknowledging her goons as I gripped my duffle and nodded toward the door, waiting for Cara. Seemed like I was always waiting on Cara.

She managed a nod, an action that took her a second to accomplish; an action that made her look unsure and nervous.

I gave her one look, catching the way the sharp glint in her eyes lessened and how her face relaxed. She was shooting for friendly, or at least, not bitchy.

That was the closest any Carelli got to friendliness. Cara wanted something. She wanted me to give it to her. I inhaled, wishing for a do-over.

Wishing like hell my path had never crossed Cara's.

A jerk of my head and I nodded toward the door, ignoring the way her mouth twitched, like she was happy I wasn't putting up a fight. "Lead the way."

Chapter Three
Kiel

There were two cars, both S-Class Mercedes, black, and not remotely subtle. One dipped with the combined weight of the two meatheads when they ambled inside. Cara sat next to me in a Benz that matched the one in front of us. At least she hadn't used the limos. That would have gotten us more attention than the quick escape we were able to make from the airport with those grunting assholes clearing a path for us.

She didn't ask where I was staying. Didn't say much at all as we pulled away from the airport and the stone-faced driver navigating the ridiculous sedan slipped into traffic, following the lead of the car ahead of us. Cara didn't speak, and I damn sure wouldn't.

But I couldn't ignore the sweet, seductive whiff of her perfume filling the cab of the car. Chanel. Rich. Tempting. A scent that had distracted me the first time I met her. The first time I'd hassled her into giving me a lead on the story I was chasing.

Outside the window, New York went by in a blur of sound and light. So much was familiar to me. So much of it made me feel like a stranger to the city I'd called home. I'd been a kid the last time I was here. I'd been a kid in love with a girl who was no good for me.

The same girl who turned her back on me and let her father send me packing, running for home like a dog with a limp. But some things hadn't changed, like the slip of the sun sinking into the river and the dance of light that reminded me of the clear, inky black night back home in Seattle. Here, you couldn't make out the stars, not like you could back home, but the skyscrapers and buildings peppered all over the city created its own kind of universe. In the center of it was that smell and the woman next to me. I told myself I hated both, and maybe, deep down, I did. But something inside me stirred and warmed when Cara shifted in her seat, leaning to her side as she did. She wore a fitted dress and three-inch heels that made those toned calves of hers flex when she stretched her feet.

I closed my eyes, trying to ignore that intense feeling that rattled my insides. It was lust, pure and simple. Cara wasn't some typical mafia princess. She fit no stereotype. She was smart, she was ruthless, and my God, she was the most beautiful woman I'd ever seen.

Kane had done well for himself. Kit was fucking stunning. Talented. Smart. But Cara was the kind of woman that made a man wish he were alone with her in the world. No woman's looks could compare to the slope of her small nose and the perpetual twist of her thick lips. She wasn't *pretty*. She wasn't *cute*. Cara was radiant, all woman, and she looked the part. She had grace. She had confidence and could lift a man up with a smile and crush him with the hint of a frown.

Little Goddess. She'd hated it when I called her that, but it was a fitting description. One I tried like hell to keep to myself.

I didn't look. Didn't acknowledge the way she leaned against her elbow, gaze moving over my profile, then down to my shoulders and chest. She was inspecting, and while she did, that sweet, *fuck me* scent came at me thicker and richer, more tempting than warm, sweet cookies from the oven.

Fuck me if I didn't want a bite.

"You look good, Kiel."

"Good" was drawn out, like Cara wasn't sure she wanted the syllables to leave her mouth, and I glanced at her, keeping silent as I threw a look her way and cocked my eyebrow up.

She exhaled, head shaking. "What? I can't compliment you?"

She wanted to keep my attention, that much I knew. Cara liked to hold center court, especially when she bothered to address you. She hated being ignored, so when I directed my focus back on the window and the city zooming by, the small grumble she released didn't surprise me.

"The last time I saw you, you looked straight in my face and told the cops I was the asshole who'd stalked you for six months." I stretched out my legs, resting an elbow on the door. "A stalker you married—"

"Kiel..."

"And fucked on the trunk of your father's limo not two hours before."

She didn't gasp or shoot a look at the driver, something that surprised me. That meant she didn't care what the man thought. That meant he wasn't her father's man.

Interesting.

"You let me come in your mouth, remember?"

That time she reacted, sitting up straight in her seat, but I knew my stroll down memory lane—and how public I made it—was pissing her off.

"It got in your hair and ended up all down your neck and—"

"Fuck's sake, Kiel, enough." Cara's shout was loud, sharp enough that it came out as a piercing echo against the windows. That small slip of composure had her face reddening, and I grinned, not hiding the small chuckle that rumbled in my throat.

Cara ignored me, leaning a little to catch the driver's attention. She gave him directions, something spoken in perfect Italian. I only recognized some of the words—park and wait—before the man pulled up in front of the hotel. My hotel. The hotel I knew my new job wouldn't have set me up in.

I whistled, the sound low. A little impressed as I stretched to the right, looking out of Cara's window and up at the building with the wavy awning lit up like New Year's Eve.

"Wow." She watched me as I sat back, ignoring her goons as they stood on either side of the car waiting, I assumed, for her signal. "Does your papa know you're dropping a grand a night on me?" She glared, nostrils flaring, and I closed my eyes, pinching the bridge of my nose. "Fuck, Cara, you orchestrated all this shit?" When she didn't answer, I dropped my hand and glared at her. "Was that interview I did all bullshit? Is the fucking job even real?"

"It could be," she promised, watching me. Waiting, I guessed, to see what other insults I had for her. When none came, she fastened the top button on her jacket and sat up, slipping off the seat belt. "Let's go inside, and we'll have a conversation. I'm not asking for a lot, Kiel, and I think you'll like what I have to say."

"That," I started as she tapped the window with a knuckle, "is very fucking unlikely."

Chapter Four
Kiel

The hotel was luxurious. I'd passed by it at least a dozen times on my way to the park when I was at school. It had been a pipe dream I'd admitted to Cara once. Stay there like a baller, like I'd just won a Pulitzer and every editor of every major magazine in the country wanted to work with me. We'd stay here and look down on the city below from the twenty-fifth floor. Our own kingdom beneath our feet.

But as I followed Cara inside, watched those tempting hips sway in front of me, I reminded myself that sometimes dreams stayed dreams for a reason. I didn't need a Pulitzer. I didn't want to be anyone's damn king, and the hotel wasn't as impressive as it had been when I was a senior in college, interning at *New York Magazine*.

For starters, nice as it was, the place was a monochromatic wet dream. Variations of dark, light, grayish, and pale beige covered the lobby from floor to ceiling. What wasn't beige or close to it was marble, with *hints* of beige or dark wood, with *tones* of beige or its cousin, greige. Occasionally, there'd be the sparkle and glitter of light overhead, but it didn't bring any color to the space or kill the color-blind sensation I got as Cara marched us to my room.

A maid waited for us at the door, holding it open as we entered. Cara walked straight to the expanse of floor-to-ceiling windows at the back of the suite and closed the curtains. The movement hid the manufactured stars made up from the buildings surrounding us that scattered light around the city. The panels didn't close completely, and a sliver of light fell across the room, casting Cara in brightness. She looked good standing there, silhouetted against the light, her curves exaggerated in shadows, her full breasts moving as she exhaled. But Cara wasn't some sweet pinup goddess promising release and surrender. She was a manipulative, greedy bitch who drew prey to her with the sway of her hips and the cock-aching slip of her tongue along her criminally full lips.

Son of a bitch.

"If you need anything at all—" the maid started, grin stretching when I winked at her.

"Thank you," Cara interrupted, nodding to the door so the maid would kill the flirting and leave.

The room was no room at all. It damn well shouldn't be for a grand a night. There was a small entry that led into a large living area. I threw down my bag and slipped off my jacket, checking out the full kitchen and wet bar. I glanced down a small walkway and into the bedroom. It was equipped with a king-sized bed and a sixty-inch TV mounted to the wall next to the windows.

"Gotta hand it to you," I started, rolling up my sleeves as I walked back into the living room, "You pulled out all the stops."

She turned then, stepping away from the window as I fell into a large chair next to the sofa. Cara moved around the room like she owned it. Posture straight, gait slow, without the slightest shake or shudder to her movements. I couldn't help watching her, appreciating the long lines of her legs and the plump curve of her ass.

"Not everything I do has an agenda," she admitted, walking to the wet bar to pull out two tumblers. She lifted one to me, eyebrows up, and when I didn't refuse the silent request, she went about fixing me a drink.

She remembered, that much I could tell. Amaretto liqueur. Scotch whisky. Cara thought she was funny, dredging up the past, making a "Godfather" because I used to do it for her. It had been a joke about her father and the dirty business he did.

"To old times," she said, offering me the glass as she held hers in her free hand. When I didn't take it, Cara tilted her head, blowing out a slow breath before she amended. She frowned, as though she'd just remembered something that irritated her. "To you almost fucking my slutty cousin Antonia at the airport." She didn't like the way I laughed at her, or how I still hadn't taken the glass to toast with her. "Fine, then. To whatever the hell you want to toast to. That better?"

I didn't answer, but I took the tumbler and closed my eyes when that bitter almond flavor hit my tongue. "So," I said, nodding to the ottoman in front of me. "What the hell do you want?"

Cara sat, resting her elbows on her knees, legs crossed at the ankles. She cupped the tumbler between her fingers and looked into the glass, like she hadn't figured out if she wanted to try staring at me or straight ahead.

"I can offer you half a million and a permanent position at *The Daily*."

This turned out to be one of those rare, *fuck-me* moments that had me stunned stupid. Cara shifted her gaze, breath held, chin uplifted as she watched me, but she didn't speak.

When she kept on watching me, not delivering the punch line, I slammed back my drink and deposited the empty tumbler on the end table to my right.

"The hell did you say?"

Cara sat up, lifting the tumbler toward her mouth, then seemed to change her mind about drinking, setting it on the floor next to her heels. "You heard me."

"Jesus, Cara, what the hell do you want? Really."

"The details aren't important enough to—"

"Nah. It doesn't work like that." I scrubbed my head as she went on watching me. "You don't get to kidnap me from the airport, throw a bunch of money at me, put me up in a luxury hotel, and then be all vague about why you want me here."

"Maybe I missed you."

"Try again," I said, not missing a beat.

She exhaled. Her bottom lip moved from the sigh and she lowered her shoulders, seeming to give up the non-disclosures. "Vinnie Marino is a forty-five-year-old expat from Sovano. My father thinks that tying his family in Tuscany to ours here will open up the doors for certain...imports. I don't happen to share my father's enthusiasm for how to get those doors open."

I leaned back, relaxing against the leather chair and watching Cara closely. She had tells, but not many. I'd managed to pick up on them while we were together. I didn't see even one of them as she spoke. No rapid blinks. No shoulder stretching or tapping her heel against the floor. Whatever Cara wanted made her desperate enough not to lie. That was deep shit for her.

"He wants you to marry this guy?"

"Yes," she said on an exhale, picking up her tumbler and downing half the drink.

"And that has what to do with me?"

She held the glass in front of her mouth, eyes sharp as she stared at me. I thought there might be something there, a quick blink that had me turning my head and focusing on her expression. Cara continued to drink, downing the rest of the Godfather before she set the glass down again, rubbing her fingers together. She took her time, seeming to consider her answer, calculate her response. That was new and unlike how she'd been when I knew her.

"Well," she started, adjusting herself on the ottoman. "We're still married. It's illegal for me to marry anyone."

My laugh was loud, sharp. I couldn't find it in me to care how rude it sounded. "Hand over the papers. I won't even ask for alimony."

"I...don't want to divorce you."

It felt like the air had gone out of the room. It was just then, with Cara's admission and the slip of calm that moved from her as she flexed her fingers into a fist, I realized how desperate she was.

I'd left New York bloodied and bruised, intending never to tie myself to a woman again. The Carellis had scared the hell out of me. I'd never wanted to fuck with any of them again. Didn't much care about still being tied legally to them. It just wasn't worth the hassle of going through with a divorce. Besides, her father didn't even know we were married. God knew what a shitstorm that would've caused if divorce papers had shown up with Cara's name on them.

But Cara, staring at me the way she did, looking annoyed and a little hopeful, had me wondering what angle she was playing here. "Why the hell not?"

"Because as long as I'm married to you, I *cannot* marry Vinnie."

This time when I laughed, it was on purpose, the sound biting and intentionally obnoxious. "Again, what's that got to do with me?"

"Kiel...please..."

I ignored her plea, still laughing as I grabbed my tumbler and stood in front of the sink at the wet bar. I swished water in the glass and filled it with two thick ice cubes and three fingers of bourbon. Fuck the memory lane drinks.

"He's bald," Cara said behind me as I downed my drink. Her voice was relaxed, but she still sounded irritated.

"Tell him to wear a hat." I shrugged, topping up my glass before I sat back down on the leather chair, knees apart with the tumbler resting on my thigh.

Cara ignored me, folding her arms as she leaned forward. "And he has horrible breath. He...slurps when he drinks and..." She paused when I laughed into my glass but didn't stop with explanations I guessed she thought I'd give a shit about. "Besides, he already has a girlfriend here. Johnny told me."

At the mention of her older brother, I glanced at her, unable to keep the glare from my face or calm the twitch I felt pulsing over my top lip.

Stay the fuck away from my little sister, he'd told me as he and his muscle bashed in my ribs.

Cara shook her head and pulled her attention to the large emerald on her right hand. A gift from her father on her twenty-first birthday. That downcast look was a distraction, something I knew she did because she wanted me to think she felt like shit for the beating I took.

"I...I don't want to marry someone who fucks other women." She took a breath, swallowing hard before she admitted, "God, I don't want to marry him at all."

The wet tumbler left a ring of moisture on my pants when I rested it there. It didn't matter. My focus was on Cara, my apparent wife, and the bullshit she wanted me to get tangled up in again.

Done that once.

Wasn't eager to do it again.

"Hate to break it to you, but your father thinks I'm a psycho stalker." I nodded at her, and the gesture brought her gaze back to me. "He's not likely to forget that shit."

"I'm going to tell him I lied." She shrugged when I squinted at her, scrutinizing her expression, not remotely convinced how that shit was supposed to work. Cara continued, seemingly unfazed by her father's temper or potential reaction. "I...already told Johnny."

A low, rumbling grunt vibrated in my throat. I took a drink, trying to clear it away. "And yet I still don't have an apology from that asshole."

Cara tapped her foot, looking nervous and irritated all at the same time. She seemed to hate the need to ask me for a favor, especially one this damn big.

"Johnny was doing what he was told."

"Maybe you should too," I told her.

"Kiel, please..."

I'd expected more whining, maybe a slip of control as she tried to keep herself in check. I was actually impressed she hadn't stomped her foot and pitched a fit when I laughed the first time, but the years appeared to have matured her. They seemed, at least, to have taught her patience. What I hadn't expected was that slow exhale of hers twisting into a groan of frustration and then a low, purring sound that I'd heard from her before.

When she played dirty.

Cara slid to the floor on her knees, inclining that long, lithe body toward me. She rested her arms against my thighs and lowered her voice. "Would it be so bad? Pretending to still love me?"

"That's what you want?" I dipped my head, pressing my palm into my eye before I groaned, staggered at the monumental shit she wanted from me. "God, Cara, I'm a good liar, but that requires some Oscar-caliber acting. I don't have those kinds of chops."

She moved slowly, leaning to the right, and I caught the curve of her breast and the way her silver chain and crucifix pendant flirted in the tempting depths of her cleavage.

"My father... He's...sick, Kiel." That she said in a whisper, low enough that I had to really listen to make out what she said.

"How sick?"

She didn't need to answer. The quick stab of pain shot across her face. A rare slip of emotion pulling down her mouth before she lifted her chin, eyes soft, tempting again as she watched me. She wanted this badly. She wanted this enough that she pushed back the hurt she felt at what would end it.

She *was* desperate.

"Why not just wait until he kicks it?" Cara frowned, and I held up my hands. "Hold out until he's gone. Johnny will take over, and you'll go about your business... And I'll try to salvage what's left of my reputation in New York."

The slow descent of her arms inching toward my thighs halted then, and Cara tilted her head, killing the sex kitten half lilt of her eyes completely. "You're staying? I mean, even if you say no, you're still staying?"

"Yeah."

I wasn't sure what to make of her expression. Surprise, for sure, maybe a little pleasure, but I wouldn't bet on it. Cara was the best actress I knew. She lied like a gambler with nothing in his hand and a million-dollar pot in front of him.

"My father isn't backing down. He's got it in his head that I need a husband before he dies. If he knows about us..."

"He did know about us, remember?" She went silent at my interruption, watching me as I sat up, forcing her back when I leaned again the armrest. "You lied to him. He had Johnny and his meatheads beat me to a pulp."

"That's because he thought you were bothering me."

"Got that backward."

"I'll tell him the truth." The purr was back, and for the first time, Cara added a sweet half smile to her seduction. It was as beautiful, as fucking tempting as it always had been, and the little shit knew it. She knew exactly how to get what she wanted. She had a multitude of tools in her arsenal. All seductive and lethal. Every single one of them I'd seen and loved.

"All you have to do is tell him that you didn't want there to be problems between me and my father, so you decided to leave me. I'll say, when you told me you were leaving, I got mad at you and lied about who you really were."

It wasn't unbelievable. Cara had been a brat back then. Maybe she still was, but her father wouldn't doubt that maneuver. It was one she practiced often, and it always got her what she wanted.

"I'll take all the blame, I promise, and after my father... After it's over, you'll have half a million dollars and your dream job. Raquel is a friend. She knows how good you are. You impressed her in that interview. It isn't an empty position. You'll get the money and the job, and when it's done, you can walk away."

"I already walked away."

"Kiel, *please* help me."

Cara never begged.

She never pleaded.

I just watched her, and the woman came closer, resting her palms on my thighs, gaze penetrating now. Serious. "It wasn't all bad between us, remember?"

I made a noise, little more than a grunt. My stomach tightened, my throat felt thick, but I was stunned quiet as Cara turned on the charm.

Fuck me, she was good at this shit.

"You always liked the way I touched you." She moved her fingers down, rubbing her palms against the sides of my legs. Her thumbs moved over the muscle of my thighs.

Her perfume wafted again when she leaned forward. My pulse quickened, seeing how sweet she could be. How that perfect face and alluring mouth moved closer and closer.

"They beat me and left me on the wet sidewalk," I told her, leaning against the headrest behind me.

"I'm sorry," she said, wincing at my words, but Cara didn't stop touching me. She came nearer still, leaning close enough now that I could make out the curve of her breasts against my arm. I froze when she kissed my neck. Her hot breath shot prickles of raised skin over my body.

"And...they broke two of my ribs."

She paused, taking her mouth from my neck. She kept her gaze on my face as she lowered, moving slowly, touch soft and teasing against my shirt.

One button and she gave me her lips, right against my chest.

Two, and I watched, shocked, helpless, and stupid as she moved her head lower.

Three buttons now and a fourth, then Cara pressed her lips to my stomach, arching up to curve her hands against my back and kiss each rib on my right side.

Hot, wicked heat filled me. She worked a spell over me. Those full, perfect lips burned each inch of skin they touched, and her hair felt silky skimming against my naked chest. Her fingers teasing my back, then slipping to the front of my stomach as she watched me was the sweetest kind of torture.

"Cara," I said through a grunt. My common sense and reason vied for control over my weak will.

"You always liked how slow I was, Kiel." She demonstrated, nibbling on one of my nipples, tugging it between her teeth. A quick hiss left my mouth, and I felt Cara smile against my skin. "Slow and sweet and so fucking hot." She licked me then, the flat of her tongue against my nipple, sliding down my chest as she pushed open my shirt. She wanted at my stomach. It was what I loved best, and she fucking knew it.

"This...it's not gonna work..."

"No?" she asked through a laugh, watching me as she kissed my stomach. Her gaze focused on me as she slipped her fingers into my waistband. She hadn't touched my cock. Not yet. But the graze of her fingertips teased me, my pants feeling tight, and it was enough to let Cara know the effect she had on me.

"This...this is how desperate you are?" I asked, slipping farther into the chair, groaning when she popped open my button and lowered my zipper.

"No, *ciccino*," she said, a laugh in her tone I knew should have insulted me. Then she took me in her hand, rubbing her thumb along the base, slipping it over the head. "*This* is how desperate I am." Then Cara took me into her hot mouth. "Shit, *bello*, I've missed this..." Then Cara showed me how much she missed me with her mouth, tongue, and the sure grip of her hand.

Fire ignited around me. My skin felt tight, unbelievably searing. And that inside-knowing that had niggled and nagged me this entire trip screamed at me to pull her off my cock. But God, it had been a long time since Cara last touched me. Years. Too long and no one had ever ripped me up inside, made me feel turned out and put together again like this woman. She touched me like she knew my body, like she remembered every inch of it. She took and sucked and gave me her mouth like she still owned it.

"Cara..." I tried, fighting the need she stoked in me. I should tell her to fuck off. I should remind her that all this was her problem. It had nothing to do with me. Cara read the tension in my arms and the tightening of my body as she redoubled her efforts.

I went stupid then, moaning like an idiot, arching against the headrest, fingers digging into the arms of the chair. She took me in deep, my dick at the back of her throat. Her soft, delicate fingers cupped my sac until I thought I might explode right there in her mouth after just a few minutes of her attention.

Stay the fuck out of New York.

It hadn't been a request Johnny made, and I guessed it hadn't come from him alone.

And stay the fuck away from my little sister, or I will fucking slit your throat.

Then the asshole laughed as he and his boys took turns beating on me.

"Stop," I told Cara, shaking my head, pushing against her shoulders. She wouldn't move and went down on me faster, sucking harder, using her fist to stroke. It took effort, more self-control than I thought I had. "Fucking stop!" My voice was loud, my grip tight.

Cara stopped, eyes rounded and wide as she looked up at me. She still had my cock in her mouth, but I made out the frown.

"Get up," I told her, grabbing her by the arm.

"Didn't you like—"

"No," I lied, not watching her as I tucked myself back into my pants.

"Kiel, I can finish you..."

Nostrils wide, I inhaled, biting back the lust that sent fire through my veins before I managed to look at her again. "Get out."

"What did you..."

Cara didn't respond to requests. I suspected that shit hadn't changed. It would have been easy to sit there and let her suck my dick. Let me come in her mouth. Let her take everything I gave her without any complaint. If I'd asked, she probably would have let me fuck her. It would have been good. It always had been with us. But then she'd have the upper hand. Then she'd have control and say-so in what I did and how I did it.

That shit wasn't going to happen.

Not the way she wanted.

Not until I had a second to weigh my options.

"Wipe your mouth," I told her, grabbing a linen napkin from the drawer in the kitchen. She stared at me when I offered it to her but didn't refuse it. Instead, Cara dried her full lips, rubbing away any trace of me. "I don't need a pity fuck or you sucking my cock to get your way. I told you, we don't work like that."

"We used to," she said, frowning as I walked to the door.

"Yeah, well, I'm not some asshole kid chasing after a sweet piece of ass."

Cara's face went red, and I saw a spark of the girl I knew in the anger that swelled in her eyes. Couldn't help thinking it made her look fucking gorgeous too.

I opened the door, waiting for her to leave, but she slammed it shut again, holding her hand against the knob. "You're my husband—"

"Saying it enough times won't make it real. You got a license. You got a memory, but fuck, Cara, that's all you're gonna get from me."

She stepped back when I grabbed the knob, looking at me like she had no idea who I was or where the hell I got the nerve to turn her down. "You want that job, and you want me." She stared at my still hard cock, grinning as she stepped close. "I know you do."

"Maybe," I said, pulling the door open again. "But maybes aren't enough for me to step back into the lion's den."

Cara laughed until I grabbed her arm and moved her into the hall. "My father isn't a lion."

"No, but you are."

There was a small whoosh of air moving her hair off her shoulder, then the low grunt of irritation as I cut her off and slammed the door in my wife's face.

Chapter Five
Cara

My father possessed power tempered by reason. It was something I'd seen from him my whole life.

Men respected him.

They wanted to be him.

He was soft-spoken but firm. Harsh when he needed to be. Tender when he could. I had never feared him. Likely never would. I loved him because he had been good to me and my brother, Johnny. He'd doted on us, especially after our mother's death when we were kids, and because he had, because we'd clung to each other through that horrible time, like everyone else who knew him, our father earned our respect.

He had a wide reach, even with his children. He had expectations for us. He had hopes for us. Dreams he wanted to come true.

They didn't always match our own.

As a kid, my dreams were selfish. I'd wanted to be a prima ballerina. I'd studied. I'd trained for years, perfecting my form, getting into the right programs, exhibiting the precise amount of discipline. In the end, it wasn't enough. I was offered a position with the ABT. There would have been travel, training, and opportunities no one else could give me. But my father had other ideas. My dreams were not his for my life.

So I packed away my ballet slippers along with my dreams and became the dutiful daughter my papa deserved. He needed me. So did my brother. It was the way of things. What choice did I have?

But sometimes, money, power, respect, and reputation aren't enough to make you happy. Sometimes even my father's expectations were too much. There were responsibilities I couldn't get away from, given who I was. I'd rebelled.

Fell in love with that beautiful boy from Seattle.

Married him in secret.

I was happy.

But then Papa started telling me I needed to think of the future. I needed to consider my role with the museum he founded and my role within the family. I knew what he'd meant. Marriage, to someone like my brother and father. Someone very different from Kiel. If they'd found out the truth about us, God only knew what would happen to him.

At first, I fought with myself about lying to Kiel. I couldn't bear hurting him. But then, out of nowhere, in some random conversation about my wild ways, my brother reminded me of what we had lost, all of us, and what we should always remember—no matter who we loved or what we wanted for ourselves, the family came first.

The family *always* came first.

Now, New York was a prison. There were no ballets for me. There was only my family and the museum. It was my responsibility to run it. It was my obligation to keep the Carelli name, at least publicly, legitimate.

Sometimes, that was hard to do.

"*Cuore mio*, here you are." Papa looked tired. He was thinner, but his skin was still olive and his eyes were dark, lit with a fire I hoped never went out.

"Papa, did you eat?" I glanced at my brother, sitting next to my father in a leather recliner, and throwing a glare his way. Johnny shook his head, frown deepening when I tilted my head. The expression on my brother's face told me all I needed to know about our father's appetite. He hadn't been interested in food, and no amount of coaxing from any of us could tempt him.

Still, I had to try.

A glance at the small table in the solarium and the empty mugs around it told me they'd already had their morning meeting. The cups were left stained by coffee and espresso. The small saucers with half-eaten muffins were scattered around the table, along with a small stack of clean dishes and flatware left by the maid next to a tray of orange juice and linens.

"I'm not hungry. Come." Papa gestured to the chair on his other side, patting the seat. "Sit. Tell me about your night with Vinnie."

I ignored the request and the low, snorting laughter Johnny released when I sat next to my father, pulling out a cannoli from my bag. The paper crinkled, and the crust flaked against the saucer when I took an empty one from the table.

"Here," I told him, offering the pastry to him. "It's from Angelo's. It's the cream cheese and ricotta ones you love so much. I got this special for you. First batch they made this morning."

Papa turned up his nose but took the frown from his face when I sighed. I used the same pout that had always gotten me out of missed curfews and unauthorized shopping sprees. "Papa, for me?"

"Ah, *mi passerotto*. Fine..." He sat up then, taking a small bite from the cannoli before he flopped back against his chair, wiping the cream cheese from his mouth with the napkin I handed him. "Now, Vinnie," he said, moving his head to rest back against the chair, his attention on me.

"Well..." I shot a glance at my brother, hoping Papa didn't catch the hard look I gave him. Johnny thought it was a bad idea telling our father about Kiel before he'd agreed. We'd need him here before I explained to my father why I couldn't marry Vinnie.

My brother cleared his throat, giving his head a shake before I could answer. I got the hint. No need for honesty. Not just yet. Papa's hand felt weak. His grip faint when I pulled on his fingers and placed his hand palm up on my leg.

"I had to cancel on Vinnie." My father curled his fingers, made like he was going to pull his hand away, but I held it tighter, smiling at him before he could complain. "I forgot I'd promised Father Russo I'd show him the new da Vinci exhibit on loan from the Vatican at the museum before the fund raiser. It's for the homeless shelter, remember?" He nodded and circled his fingers around mine. "Anyway, Vinnie will be out in Philadelphia this weekend, I think he said, so we'll get together next week if our schedules mesh."

"Don't keep putting him off, *bella*." My father patted my hand but kept his expression stern, as though he wanted me to understand the importance of what he had to say. "He's a patient man, but you shouldn't keep your attention from him too much. He'll think you're not interested."

Johnny caught my gaze again, rustling his paper as if to keep me from complaining to my father about the disgusting asshole he wanted me to marry. Papa had bad cataracts. His vision was horrible. But even a blind man could see Vinnie's true colors.

Sadly, my father didn't.

Maybe it made me petty and superficial to complain about Vinnie's belly or his baldness, but I couldn't help myself. There wasn't anything about him I found remotely attractive. There was no way I could attach myself to him for life—something I knew my father would expect—if there was zero spark between us. I could get past the baldness, maybe even the paunch he carried. But his obnoxious bragging and the way he treated people was too much. He was an asshole, and I couldn't stand him.

But my father had ideas.

He had plans.

He saw Vinnie as an asset. Someone to help Johnny run the business after he...well. In the future. Vinnie never showed his true self to my father. He wasn't stupid, and because he wasn't, I was going to have to marry him. Unless, of course, Kiel would agree to back me up.

God, I prayed he would.

"She knows, Papa," Johnny said, standing when the maid entered the room. My brother leaned against my chair, nudging my shoulder as if he wanted me to agree with him. "Cara is smart. She knows what a catch Vinnie is." He lifted his eyebrows, a silent request for me to agree.

"Of course I do." I forced a smile, staring unblinking at my father as he watched us.

"Excuse me, Mr. Carelli," Eliza, the housekeeper, interrupted. "Dr. Michaels is here for your appointment."

Papa waved his hand, dismissing the woman. I stood anyway, bending down to kiss my father's forehead. "Be nice to her," I told him when he started to argue. "She's a good woman."

"So are you, *cucciola*," my father told me, squeezing my hand before the short doctor in the tailored suit came through the door, Eliza trailing behind him.

"We'll see you later, Pop." Johnny nodded toward the door when Eliza and the doctor helped my father away from the table.

My brother had me by the arm, leading me down the long hallway toward the kitchen. The house was massive, at least six thousand square feet, with marble tile on every surface and fountains in the center of the colossal circular drive. We moved through ornate plaster archways and into the small alcove between the sunroom and the breakfast nook before Johnny uttered a sound.

"So?" he asked, as though that would be enough for me to get his meaning.

"What? Papa looks bad, and you need to make sure he eats whenever you're with him." I curled my arms tight, holding back the urge to smack Johnny on the back of the head. He knew better than to let our father beg off eating.

"He does look bad, and we're handling it. I told Eliza this morning we'll have to bring in a new dietician. I'll talk to Michaels about what we can do to increase his appetite." Johnny looked over his shoulder when Eliza moved down the hall, heading toward the pantry. My brother led me into the sunroom, shutting the glass door behind us. "Did you see your *husband*?"

The last word came out through gritted teeth. I shook my head, wondering if my brother would ever manage to grow up. I could have married Giorgio Armani, and the idiot would complain about my man being in the fashion industry. No one would ever measure up in Johnny's eyes.

"I did. I made the offer."

Johnny frowned, head tilting as though he expected more of an explanation.

"What?"

"*Cazzo,* Cara. What the hell did he say?"

"He kicked me out." I didn't bother mentioning I was in the middle of *something* when Kiel got rid of me. That was too humiliating to relive.

Johnny flared his nostrils, scratching his chin as he looked out the window. I understood his irritation. When I first confessed the truth about my marriage to Kiel, my brother had been livid. But then Papa announced he wanted me to marry Vinnie, and any real anger Johnny felt toward me were squashed. He'd seen Vinnie for who he was and wasn't interested in letting the asshole in on our family business.

"Well," Johnny grunted, nodding to himself like there was something he needed to work out on his own. "Be that way," he said, pulling his cell out of his pocket, then ordering a quick, "Bring me my Caddy," before he ended the call.

"What the hell do you think you're doing?" I asked him, hurrying to follow when he brushed me off. "Johnny, don't you dare..."

"I'll take care of it," he promised, moving ahead of me. His stride was longer, his movements quicker with those long legs of his.

"You better not—"

"Miss Cara," Eliza said, stepping next to me as Johnny continued down the long hallway. I shot a glance at the housekeeper but kept my attention on my brother's retreating back. "Your father wants to see you about the fund raiser."

"I'll come back when—"

"I think Dr. Michaels would like a word with you and your brother before you both..." She stopped talking when Johnny left through the front door. "Well. You then," she said, motioning me away from my brother and toward the entrance leading to the solarium. "He really was very insistent."

"Oh...okay," I told her, finally looking away from the closed door to follow behind Eliza.

My steps were quick, my heartbeat thudding, and I said the smallest prayer, hoping the day wouldn't end with Johnny and Kiel trying to kill each other. I wasn't so sure that prayer would get answered or who would come off worse when it was all over.

Chapter Six
Cara

Kiel liked coffee—thick, rich coffee with cream and two sugars. He liked dark roast. None of those café or breakfast blends.

Once, he'd told me, he spent a month in New Orleans his sophomore year doing an internship on the crime beat. He'd fallen in love with rich coffee then, promising nowhere he'd been in the world had coffee as good as the Louisiana roasts he drank in New Orleans.

The cup in front of him was likely a poor substitute, but Kiel still sipped it, looking relaxed. He looked more in control than I'd ever seen him as Johnny sat across the table from him. It was an outdoor gourmet coffee shop that sold all variations of coffee along with specialty chocolate and was just a few blocks from Kiel's hotel. I'd been here once before. They had good blends.

At the moment, though, I didn't care about how good the coffee was. My only concern was getting my brother away from Kiel without the cops across the street or the kids at the table next to them getting caught up in whatever drama there would be.

And God, I knew there would be drama.

They sat only ten feet from me, just around the corner of the building. I could make out most of the conversation. It seemed, from what I heard, to be a game of insults delivered through mock calm and smooth smiles, none of which were sincere. The last they'd seen each other, Johnny and his boys were pulverizing Kiel's body.

"Is it the money?" Johnny asked, his tone curious but still calm.

"I don't need your money or hers." Kiel wasn't loaded. That much I'd found out when I had the PI check what he'd been up to. His background came back clear, and his work at the *Seattle Times* was proof enough that he was doing okay, but not remarkably well, writing on the crime beat.

"You're too proud," Johnny said, moving in his chair, the metal feet scraping against the cement below him. "You and my sister, you're both too damn proud."

"Your sister and I, as those pronouns work together, aren't any of your business."

"That," Johnny said, voice slipping lower, "is where you're wrong." His voice that deep, his words that enunciated, signaled his anger. My big brother was getting pissed. It was never good when that happened.

"Let me paint you a scenario, Carelli. Just to recap, so we're clear."

Kiel never let his voice falter. The inflection didn't rise. He didn't get irritated and let his tone become clipped. He maintained his calm, not giving away any indication of his mood. It was a talent he'd always had, but as he continued speaking, I realized it was one talent he'd perfected.

"Five years ago, I chased down a lead. Money for the Bolton Mission not receiving all their donations. How the mission had seen a five percent drop in its output to the homeless community because of the missing donations. Donations raised by your father's museum. Donations received when the new museum director, your little sister, took over. I go to the source, find out what I need to know from your sister. She's more than willing to hand over her books to prove she wasn't responsible."

Kiel's chair squeaked as he spoke, and he moved one hand as he continued. It was his only tic, the only thing that made his control slip, if just a bit. "It was a fluff piece given to me by a bored editor who wanted the intern out of his hair. I was eager. Desperate to make an impression. But I fucked up, like most kids do. I forgot to separate myself from the story. I forgot that the source should stay a source. The next thing I knew, your sister was at my apartment, in my bed, telling me everything I wanted to hear about how smart I was. How far I could go. All, I'm sure, to keep me off the story."

Something sharp rattled in my chest, and my stomach dipped. Kiel thought I'd been responsible? He thought I'd taken money from the mission? How did I never know that?

"You think my sister stole from homeless people?" Johnny asked, his tone a little amazed.

"I think there are a lot of homeless people who got shafted when your sister was put in charge of the fund raiser. I know I did because even though she promised she loved me, even though she went as far as saying 'I do' when I convinced her to marry me, I still ended up accused of being a fucking stalker. My night ending with you and your meatheads beating my ribs in." Kiel took a long sip of his coffee, his movements slow, his attention never leaving Johnny's face. "Now she's coming back around, asking me to pretend that she never lied about me or that you are accepting, sincere, and expect me to forget. I flew home to my people with broken ribs and a bloody face, all because your kid sister didn't want your old man to know she'd lifted a hundred grand from a mission catering to folks without a pot to piss in."

"Hell, man, you gotta learn to let shit go."

In the reflection on the window to my right, I spotted Kiel's expression. His mouth was set so straight and hard, his lips nearly disappearing behind his frown. Then he inhaled, shifting the line of his mouth into a half smirk. I stood away from the building, ready to pounce between them if they started fighting. That look on Kiel's face was dangerous.

The half smirk stayed, and Kiel relaxed against his chair, leaning on his left elbow as he lifted his chin at my brother. "You ever forget about the fucker who took out your cousin Michael?"

I held my breath, trying not to curse at Kiel for the reminder. Michael had been a kid. Just twenty and under Johnny's wing, wanting to learn the business at my brother's side. But Ralphie Rizzo, a stupid kid from Newark, got it in his head that taking Michael out would clear the way for him at Johnny's side. A bullet to Michael's temple had nearly ruined my brother.

Johnny's jaw worked, his eyes narrowing so small, I could hardly make out the whites in them before he shook his head.

"Never." My brother shifted his hard stare, looking at Kiel like he was impressed. Probably unhappy that Kiel'd found out about Michael, but still impressed that he had.

Kiel shrugged, dismissing Johnny's unspoken demand that he explain how he knew about the murder. "I'm a journalist, and your family fucked me over. You think I don't watch my back?"

Johnny nodded, and the heat in his face dimmed.

Kiel didn't relax his tight shoulders or loosen the stiffness in his arms, but when he spoke again, his tone was back to normal. "You won't forget that asshole, and I won't forget you or your sister. Kind of hard when it's tied up in promises I meant when I made them."

"You loved her."

I released the breath I held when he answered, "Point is, I don't now."

Tired of the back-and-forth, I pushed away from the building and approached the table, glaring at my brother when he shot his attention to me. "I told you I'd handle this," he said, nodding to Kiel.

"Uh-huh. It sounds like you've done a bang-up job." I didn't bother to look at Kiel when he coughed over his low laughter. Instead, I nodded toward the two guards near the sidewalk, both my brother's men. "Papa needs you, and I need to have a conversation with Kiel."

"Cara, you really shouldn't..."

Johnny went silent, frowning when I glared at him, my nostrils flaring. I suspected he knew what I'd say. "Calling in my freebie."

"Cara, this isn't the time—"

"Sammy Nicola."

Johnny grunted. He cursed under his breath before he exhaled, pushing back from his chair to stand. He reached into his pocket, drew out a fifty, and threw it on the table before he nodded at Kiel.

"Trust me on this, you think she was stubborn back then? She's gotten a fuckton worse. Do the thing. Get your money and get it over with, or she'll be on your balls forever."

He nodded again at Kiel and ignored me completely. Then he left with his two guards, heading down the sidewalk.

I didn't wait for Kiel to ask me to sit. If I was going to discuss anything with him, I didn't want to wait.

"Kiel—"

"Who's Sammy Nicola?" he asked, sounding amused, as though he hadn't just asked me to reveal my brother's most shameful secret. When I only watched him, head angled as I squinted, Kiel laughed. "You want me to get back in bed with your family. Maybe I wanna have something on your brother. Call it a good-faith request."

I hesitated only for a second before I motioned the waitress over, pointing to Kiel's cup and shooting two fingers at her. "Samantha Nicola," I said, looking back at my husband. I still couldn't shake the insult I felt at the revelation he made to Johnny, how he thought I was capable of stealing from a mission. But then, if I were Kiel, I suppose I wouldn't put anything past me either. Didn't mean the sting wasn't there. "Seventeen-year-old niece of my father's favorite priest. Beautiful girl."

"He knock her up?" Kiel asked, sending a smile of thanks to the waitress when she delivered our coffee.

Around us, the group of kids finished up their iced coffee and headed down the sidewalk. There were people ambling by, like they didn't see anyone or anything, and even the cops across the street had moved on. Right then, I was the only one holding Kiel's attention.

"Took her virginity." The coffee was rich, like I guessed, and I added three sugars and one cream to the mug to get the taste right. "She was set to go to St. Agnes that fall. Something she and her uncle had planned since she was ten. And then...well, Johnny happened."

"I take it the priest found out."

I nodded, remembering how freaked-out Johnny had been. Across the table, Kiel rolled his eyes, downing his coffee like it was water.

"And your father..."

"Still doesn't know. Sammy decided she was in love with Johnny, and when the priest confronted him and demanded he marry the girl since he'd already taken her virtue, my brother paid them both off. Donations to the church for the insult and to the convent for the loss of their potential sister. Sammy didn't feel worthy enough to go into the calling after that. It cost Johnny a lot. The priest told him he was a worthless Catholic who shamed his father's good name and our mother's precious soul by touching someone so pure and innocent. It was like a curse to Johnny. He said if our father ever found out, he'd up and join a monastery himself. Claims it's his greatest shame."

Kiel laughed behind his cup. "Like they'd take him."

"Exactly what I told him."

He watched me then, focused on my gaze. Did he feel the zip between us, that slow, barely there hum of chemistry shooting from my gaze to his? It wasn't my imagination. I knew he wanted me. Last night was proof enough of that, but this was something more. Simple. Brief, but it was still there.

The thing, whatever it had been between us all those years ago, was still present. I knew I wasn't imagining it.

"Last night..." I started, but I didn't finish as Kiel shook his head, moving his shoulders down as though he was disappointed.

"Last night won't be repeated."

"Because you aren't going to help me?" He didn't answer, deciding, it seemed, to keep his thoughts and his answer to himself. I used the silence and his hesitation to my advantage, pulling out my purse. The clasp gave way when I opened it, and Kiel watched me as I took out the envelope and slid it across the table. "It's yours if you want it." I nodded at it. "That's half. The rest comes after..." I trailed off on the rest of my explanation, knowing Kiel caught my meaning. "The job, though, it's yours if you want it. Tomorrow. This afternoon. Just say the word."

He picked up the envelope but didn't open it. Instead, Kiel folded it in half, tapping the corner on the table as he watched me. I remembered that look— the down slip of his eyelids and the squint they moved into. The pinched corner of his mouth as he thought, considered everything he deemed worthy of weighing and sorting before he decided. It could last seconds, hours for the big decisions.

"Just like that," he said finally, laying the envelope flat with his large hand over it. "Write a check, buy a husband, buy your way clear from a man you find repulsive."

"It's not that simple." He didn't think much of me, I knew that, but not all that long ago, Kiel had known me better than anyone. I wasn't petty. Despite my response and description of Vinnie, I wasn't shallow. "He only wants me because he wants my father's... business."

"Johnny has that."

"Yeah, well, this isn't exactly a business where obstacles stay obstacles for long."

"Shit." Kiel blew out a breath, abandoning the check and the table altogether as he ran his fingers through his hair. "Right back where I was again. That's what you're thinking? That I'm fine getting mixed up with you again?"

What could I say? That's exactly what I wanted. That was what I needed to protect myself and my father's company.

It wasn't fair.

It wasn't easy, but that was the truth.

I decided that's what Kiel deserved from me.

"I need you to protect me."

Something shifted in his expression then. The irritated worry that wrinkled Kiel's forehead smoothed out. "What do you mean?"

"I'd never ask unless it was important to my family. After...Michael, we've had to watch ourselves." I moved closer, leaning on my elbows and lowering my voice. "My father is sick and getting sicker. He's not thinking clearly. He's not thinking at all. He's worried he'll die and I'll be left alone with only Johnny to watch after me. But Johnny will be...taking over. He'll have other things to occupy his attention. Papa doesn't want me to be left unguarded. If you came back, after I explained, after I told him the truth, then he'd be easy, I think. He'd realize what a bad idea Vinnie in our family is."

Kiel laughed but didn't seem amused. "Cara, I'm a big, Protestant Samoan from Seattle. I'm not white. I'm not Catholic, and I damn sure am not Italian. You think your father is gonna welcome me with open arms?"

"If he thinks I love you, yes. He will." I let my breathing settle, unused to the scrutiny Kiel was giving me. I knew what he was thinking. There likely wasn't much good in his head about me. There was likely even less belief that I could fake loving him. I saw the thoughts in his expression and did my best to ignore them. "None of that other stuff will matter as long as I'm... happy."

"You're that good of an actor?" Kiel asked, face coming closer, and I wondered if he moved nearer on purpose. I wondered if he'd ever believed me if I told him the truth.

"I can be believable," I said, ignoring the question.

"Don't I fucking know it."

There was no point trying to convince him. He had the check. He had my offer, and if I sat at that table any longer, Kiel's face, his wide, wild eyes, would have me begging to get back to where we were last night.

I'd had his cock in my mouth, getting off myself on hearing the way he moaned. How he loved the way I sucked him, the way I hummed against his skin. The power was overwhelming. The pleasure he'd gotten was a high of its own.

Then he'd kicked me out and took away the small connection I'd offered him. That hurt almost as much as his thinking I was a thief.

"You let me know what you decide, please," I said, standing from the table. I pushed down my skirt, unwilling to look at Kiel again. It had been too much. "I can't put off Vinnie or my father forever, so we're on a time crunch."

No goodbyes. No more pleas. I walked away from Kiel, knowing he was watching me, feeling the heavy fire that burned my skin from his sharp gaze.

I'd taken five steps, was nearly to the sidewalk, when Kiel called after me. "Hey, Cara, what's your greatest shame? You deflower a priest in training?"

I stopped, glancing at him over my shoulder. "No priests in training," I started, looking him over, a deep wrinkle pinching between my eyebrows. "I broke the heart of this big, Protestant Samoan. Worst damn thing I've ever done."

I turned and walked away before he could respond. Before I thought too long about the look he'd given me at my confession. I couldn't let myself believe it was anything but my imagination telling me what that look meant. It looked a lot like love, but Kiel Kaino would never look at me like that.

Not me.

Not ever again.

Chapter Seven
Kiel

Her walk took talent.

It wasn't a strut. It wasn't a trot. Cara Carelli was a fucking glider. She moved her hips as though there was a constant rhythm sounding in her head and her body danced to it without her knowing. Small, tiny waist. Round, perfect ass and legs that went on for days and days, as if there was time enough in the world for her to get anywhere she wanted to go.

It was those gliding movements I'd watched as she walked away after delivering a confession I'd half convinced myself was utter horseshit.

I broke the heart of this big, Protestant Samoan. Worst damn thing I've ever done.

That was the aforementioned shit. Cara was a Carelli, and that meant she never apologized for a fucking thing. Guilt was a commodity for the weak, and Cara was a damn strong woman. But there had been something in her eyes. It was the low, dark cast of some emotion I couldn't quite make out.

She'd changed a lot—or maybe she hadn't changed at all and I was only just finding out who she really was. Everything before with us had been wild and manic and so damn fast. I'd jumped from the cliff's edge, chasing after that beautiful girl, forgetting about the jagged rocks that waited for me in the water.

I knew regret. I knew what it looked like and how hard it could shift expressions. How tight and worried it made you look. Cara's emotion had been raw, evident, and was something I remembered. It was something I'd looked at every day in the mirror when I did yet another dumb-shit thing. Did that a hell of a lot the past five years.

It was that look that stuck with me, long after I finished watching the glide she pulled off down the sidewalk.

"Fucking talent," I'd told no one in particular, laughing to myself as my wife walked away.

Then I'd left the coffee shop and walked to the park, taking in the tourists and the places we'd called our own forever ago. It was stupid to think about those days—how we'd been half crazed with lust, rolling around on a blanket under a low-hanging elm tree. Or hiding behind the heavy pink flowers of a Japanese magnolia, kissing and touching because that's what you did when you were in love. That's what you did when you thought it would go on forever and ever, and you wanted all that shit to start right then.

The walk had done nothing to clear my head. Neither had the four glasses of bourbon or the half hour of porn I tried watching when I got back to my room. At least it was high-dollar shit. Great production quality, but the woman bent over a kitchen counter had the same complexion as Cara. Round, dark eyes hidden behind an inch of eyeliner. She was made-up, fake. She wasn't graceful. She wasn't mysterious. I'd given up trying to get my wife off my mind and downed the rest of the bourbon, then spent the remainder of the night and all the next day ignoring Kane's calls and the half-dozen texts from Cara.

Please, she'd written. *I need an answer.*

That had been the last one. I woke up this morning, staring at the message and the others like it, trying like hell to remind myself how much I hated her.

I owed that bitch nothing.

She was slick, smooth, and knew just how beautiful she was. Cara, like her father and brother, was manipulative and shrewd, only caring about people when they had something to offer.

It was the only reason I got their attention now.

She *needed* me.

"Fuck that," I said to the empty room, groaning over the incessant pounding happening in my head.

The bathroom was clean. The walk-in shower massive. All marble tile with a massive rainwater shower head up top and six jets surrounding the walls. I tapped the cold water and amped up the hot before I jumped under all those sprays, leaning my arms against the farthest wall.

I wanted to drown myself. I wanted to get lost in the sensation of the scorching water and the steady pound of those pulsing sprays as they moved over my head, down my neck, and over my chest and back. I didn't want to think about Cara and her thick, full lips. I didn't want to remember how tight her mouth felt around my cock when she sucked me off the other night.

"Shit." The mutter was low, barely audible over the pounding water, and it got squashed behind the low grunt of irritation I couldn't keep in my throat. Flashes of Cara kneeling in front of me shot through my head.

The tile was cool on my forehead when I leaned against it, cursing my disloyal body for the reaction it had to those flashes. Her mouth had been tight. Her tongue soft and warm, nearly as powerful as her fingers. She worked my cock like she always had—like she was a woman who knew how to please her man.

"Fuck."

My dick got harder then. I pushed off the tile, flattening one hand against the wet shower wall as I gripped my cock in my free hand. "To hell with it," I groaned, giving up the weak effort I'd put up trying to keep hate and anger brimming hotter than the memory of Cara's mouth and tongue and sweet, full lips.

It wouldn't take long, I knew that. My fingers were tight. My strokes even and perfect as I worked my cock over and over, letting my head get thick with images of Cara's mouth and body and the flawless contours of her face. She had me the other night, right in her hands. She could have asked for anything if I hadn't pushed her away.

But then, Cara had always known how to touch me. She'd been the only one to ever read me and know what I wanted, what worked to get me weak.

With my fist pumping faster, the memories shifted and went deeper until I recalled one Sunday afternoon in my old apartment. It had been summer. July, I think.

The windows were open, the sun barely a blip of light against the dark sky around the city. Cara slept against my chest, her full breasts touching my ribs. Her long, smooth legs twisted between mine. She'd smelled like something sweet, reminding me of wild grass and mint. Scents I knew from the soaps and lotions my mother had always made when we were kids. She was too poor for store-bought products like that, and when I'd admitted to having a girlfriend, my mother had sent Cara a care package—homemade lotion, soap, and a few loaves of her banana bread. I'd thought Cara would turn up her nose at the care package, but she'd fallen in love with everything.

We'd eaten the breads in under a week and had spent that summer weekend bathing each other in the rest.

It had felt good, holding her, feeling the weight of her body against mine, my own wrecked and sore, and a fucking smile on my face I couldn't get rid of. There'd been the faint noise of a siren in the distance that morning and the low hum of the fan oscillating on the stand. Then Cara smiled against my chest and rubbed her nose against my ribs, humming through a yawn as she sat up to straddle me. She looked surreal. Her naked body shadowed by the peek of light but still visible, all that sweet perfection mine for the taking.

"I could stay here with you always, Kiel." She'd stretched, back arching and breasts moving up, then slowly down as she adjusted on top of me.

I moved my hands up, smoothing over her waist, to her ribs, and higher to cup her ample breasts. I sat up and teased them, loving the purring hum Cara released and smiling to myself when that hum became a moan.

"Then let's stay," I told her, my voice low, a little awed. She was real and there and mine. "Stay with me inside this room. We can forget the world outside."

"How long would that last?" she asked, curling her long arms around my shoulders.

"Forever."

"Forever isn't real, cuore mio." She lowered her shoulders, trying to pull away. I stopped her, holding her face between my hands. "What?"

"Forever is real if you want it to be." I'd held my breath. The thought of her leaving wrecked something inside me. I didn't think. I didn't reason. I just said the first thing that came to me. The thing I wanted and meant but only knew I did when I spoke the words. *"Marry me. Right now. Today."* She went completely still, and I took her silence as the chance I needed to convince her. *"I love you, Little Goddess. We'll make our forever start right now."*

I never knew what went through her head as she watched me, eyes impossibly wide, bottom lip trembling as I waited for her to turn me down. The *no* I expected seemed to die on her tongue as she went on looking at me. Probably debating with herself how she'd landed in bed with an impulsive asshole who didn't think before he spoke. The same asshole who didn't regret the proposal after it left my mouth.

But Cara didn't say no. She didn't ask why I wanted her. After the longest ten seconds of my life, that beautiful woman closed her mouth, blinking her eyes like something was stuck between her lashes.

"Yeah," she'd said finally, kissing me lightly, hand to my cheek as my chest tightened. I was sure my heart had gotten too big for my chest. Cara was calm, the smile she wore genuine, and she nodded, inhaling deeply, like she wanted to keep the moment inside her and not miss a single detail. *"Yeah, Kiel. Let's do it. You and me and a million forevers."*

That memory was sweet. It didn't make me hate Cara. It reminded me why I never really could, no matter what she'd done to me. That recall, that summer day and how we'd been together...even that got tied up in wanting her, in needing something to push me over the edge. Then the memory went deeper, turned hotter. I pumped my dick faster, feeling the slip of composure, the sweet ache of release rising.

I remembered Cara above me that morning, riding me, squeezing me from the inside. She'd held on to my shoulders, clamping and bouncing and giving me every sweet inch of herself before she crashed. I pulled her down onto the mattress, and Cara's low whisper went right in my ear and straight to my chest.

"I love you too," she'd said, and just then, my world went sideways.

That was the part of the memory that stung the most. The part I couldn't get rid of. It stuck to me like a scar, deep and jagged. Right there in that luxury shower, the water pounding in time with my fist, and I came in minutes. My head was on my forearm now as I finished myself off, feeling stupid, weak, and confused about what was real and what I wanted to believe.

She hadn't meant it, I reminded myself, my body settling from the strong spin of orgasm as I turned off the water and stepped onto the bathroom floor, scrubbing a towel over my body.

Cara had never been real for me. She'd never been honest. I knew now those *I love yous* were nothing more than bullshit she said to keep me from finding out what she'd done with those donations.

No way would I help her now.

She didn't deserve it.

I kept repeating those truths as I toweled off and went into my room. I stared at my closet and the one pair of jeans and single button-up I'd brought with me. No way would I do anything for her. Never again. Not after how she'd played me.

You and me and a million forevers.

"Fuck," I whispered, cursing myself for being so weak.

I need you to protect me.

That she'd said with something close to worry. Maybe a little hesitancy pulling at her features. She hadn't wanted to admit that to me but did it anyway. Fuck me, Kane wasn't the only Kaino who was a sucker for a woman in need.

I grunted, ignoring the scream inside my own head as I dressed, brushed my teeth, and left the suite, focused on the elevator in front of me and cab ride I was about to take.

Chapter Eight
Cara

My father was sick, not helpless. He might not be as together as he once had been, but he knew his own mind. He also knew his business. Right then, with him sitting in that leather chair, a watered-down tumbler of scotch in his hand, it was business—my business—that he wanted to know more about.

"Tell me, then. Why haven't you seen him?"

Vinnie.

It was always about Vinnie lately.

My father's mind might be dulled a little by the medicine and liquor filling his veins, but he still had his faculties. He hadn't forgotten what he wanted me to do.

"Papa," I started, thinking the pout might work again. It had melted his heart when he'd asked about

Vinnie and the date I'd canceled with him. He'd warned me not to put off the man for too long. Since Kiel had come back to the city, I'd stopped answering Vinnie's calls altogether. My focus wasn't on him, my father, or any plans either of them had for me.

It was steady on Kiel. On his mouth and sarcastic grin and that glorious, sweet cock I wanted back between my fingers.

I tilted my head, coming to kneel next to my father. He kept his attention on his glass, staring blankly at the ice cubes. He did that sometimes when he was disappointed. By the message he'd left on my phone this morning, the one that simply said, "Come. There is a problem," I knew he was disappointed. I could tell by that cold, bitter tone and the low grumble in his voice.

My father never beat us. He didn't spank or ever touch us to hurt us. His words, though, wounded deep and bit hard, and that somber look of disgust and disappointment was something I'd never been able to stomach for long.

It was that look he gave me right now as he swirled the scotch around his tumbler and said, "Why don't you tell him?" He tightened the grip on his glass. He still wore his wedding ring, though it had been fifteen years since my sweet mother had died.

For Papa, for many men of his generation, you married for longer than life. He wanted everyone to know he was still loyal to her.

The click of shoes on the marble floor announced Vinnie's arrival, and I glanced over my shoulder, cursing myself for waiting on Kiel to save me. It had been stupid to expect him to show. He hadn't answered even one of my texts or messages since I'd last seen him. No surprise he hadn't made an appearance today.

This was a conversation I should have had with my father years ago. The truth had been buried under worry, resentment, and years of denying that I'd actually loved Kiel. That loving him and marrying him without my father's blessing or approval was one disappointment he'd never get over.

I'd disobeyed him by rebelling. I'd fallen for a man he'd never approve of without a lot of gentle persuasion and months, if not years, of patient introductions and conversations. That Kiel was in the damn media would have precluded him from even being introduced to my papa. Now? *Cazzo*, it was too late.

"*Ciao, bella*," Vinnie said, nodding once as he flopped onto my father's tufted sofa, fingering the gold Zippo in his hand. He stretched an arm along the back of the sofa, grinning at me as though he was pleased to have a front seat to what would end up a gigantic family squabble. "Your Papa says you want to tell me something?"

I stood then, pushing down my skirt as I forced a smile on my face. "Vinnie," I started, folding my arms tightly over my chest. He watched me, attention on my legs, pausing over my hips before his eyes went straight to my breasts. That's where his gaze stayed, only moving to my face for a few seconds at a time. That disgusting grin he wore went wicked, and I had to push back the urge to smack it from his face.

"Cara, explain to us," my father said, moving his glass between himself and Vinnie. "Tell us why you've been avoiding Vincent's attention."

The man in question leaned forward, that Zippo opening and closing as he fingered it. The bright light overhead sent a glare across his bald head. He rested his elbows on his knees, and his shirt tightened around his waist, exaggerating the paunch of his gut. "*Sì*, Cara. You don't like me? I'm not *bello* enough for you, eh?"

"Papa," I tried again, ignoring Vinnie and his stupid question. But that quick disappointment hardened my father's mouth, pulled it into a line that no amount of my pouting could erase.

"I give. You take. You are spoiled, like your brother, but I am a rich man. I have given you a good life, and I ask this small thing of you." He gestured to Vinnie, head shaking. "And you disrespect me by ignoring what I want for you. Why, *mi passerotto*? Why do you hate your Papa so?"

"You know I love you," I told my father, kneeling back down next to him. The hurt that clouded his dark eyes stung worse than the disappointment that hadn't moved from his features. It broke my heart to be the source of this. "On Mamma's grave—" I grabbed the crucifix around my neck, kissing it before I crossed myself "—you know I would never intentionally disrespect you."

For a second, my father relented. He reached forward to touch my face. I swear I caught the lower mutter of "Theresa," my mother's name, before Vinnie cleared his throat, and my father's attention went to him.

"I called, Cara." Vinnie's gaze was downcast as he fiddled with that damn lighter. "I sent flowers too. Pink roses the day after you canceled our date, sì? Red and white the days after to let you know I thought of you all that weekend. And still...*niente*. No word. No thank you."

I'd sent all of them to the hospital, to the geriatric ward. They'd appreciate them more than I would.

Vinnie lifted his chin at my father. "I know *Signore* Carelli raised dutiful children. Children with manners."

"There wasn't time for—"

"And all I'm trying to do by persuing you," Vinnie interrupted, rising from the sofa, "is to make your father happy." He stood with his hands in his pockets, gaze on my face, watching closely as I stood. When Johnny entered the room, Vinnie kept his focus on me, not bothering to acknowledge my brother. Instead, he flicked the Zippo in his pocket, the noise irritating. "Our two families would make great business..."

"I'm not interested in—"

"That doesn't really matter, does it?" Vinnie said, finally turning to look at Johnny when he came to my side.

I grabbed my brother's wrist when he stood in front of me, like Vinnie had crossed a line and Johnny would call him out on it.

"*Figlio*," Papa said, a warning in his tone. "This isn't your business."

"Yeah, Pops. It is…"

"Stop," I told my brother, pulling him to my side. "I can fight my own battles."

That made Vinnie tilt his head and my father clear his throat, like neither man understood how seriously I took their ideas about my life, or how disgusted I was by those ideas.

"We're in a battle, *bella*?" Vinnie's tone was light, amused, and the urge to smack him only intensified.

"Cara…" my father warned.

I inhaled, straightening my shoulders as I watched my father, ignoring how hard Vinnie's expression had gotten or how he'd taken a half step toward me.

"I can't marry anyone, Papa. I'm sorry."

"Why?" Vinnie asked for my father.

It was Papa I answered, eyes squeezed tight as I blurted out, "Because I'm already married."

There was no sound in the room for an entire minute. Even my father's mildly labored breathing went quiet as he watched me. The disappointment shifted into several different emotions I recognized.

Confusion, because I'd always been such a dutiful daughter. At least, as far as he knew, I had. Worry, that I'd somehow messed up my life without asking him for help to get out of it. And finally, anger that he'd been so easily fooled. I'd seen those expressions before, most of the time when Papa yelled at one of his men or at my brother when he'd fucked something up.

But never had those looks been meant for me. Now they were, and I wasn't sure I could take more of them, though I knew they were coming.

When the quiet seemed to overwhelm him, Papa exhaled, the long, slow breath moving from his nostrils. "And *who* is your husband?" His tone was calm but cold.

Johnny moved closer, pulling on my sleeve with his long fingers as though he meant to back me up. One glare from my father and my brother dropped my hand.

I made sure to look my father directly in the eye. Chin lifted, I tried to keep any emotion off my face. Showing weakness wouldn't help my situation. "Kiel Kaino," I admitted, keeping my mouth relaxed.

Anger swelled and brimmed, reddening Papa's face. "*Prendere in giro,*" he said, the sentence coming out in an astounded breath.

"No, Papa." I shook my head, ignoring Vinnie as he backed away from us and walked to the bay window at the back of the room. I kept my gaze on my father's red face, counting the seconds until he'd release his fury. "I'm not fooling around. I'm serious."

"Sei impazzita?"

"I'm not insane," I promised him, grateful when Johnny squeezed my hand again. "I'm...I'm married. To Kiel. We have been for five years."

Then my father released a litany of cursing and Italian phrases that made the hair on my arms stand on end. I was convinced by his reaction, by that rage that bellowed around the room, that my father wasn't sick at all. No one as terminal as the doctor promised could curse and fuss and carry on the way Papa did.

"How?" he kept asking over and over, not listening when I tried to explain.

"I lied to you, Papa. I was angry because Kiel didn't want there to be bad blood between our families. He told me he was going to leave until you knew the truth because of how we snuck off to get married without your blessing—"

"Che palle!" my father yelled, ignoring my desperate words and how I kept trying to touch him or keep my voice from sounding weak. He only heard the words "lied" and "snuck off." At least, those were the phrases he kept repeating back to me in Italian.

I continued, raising my voice to be heard over his ranting. "I was so mad at him for leaving that I told you I didn't know him and swore to the cops he was a stalker. It was so...stupid and..." "Why? Why would you keep such a thing from me?"

"Because I asked her to," a voice sounded, deeper, stronger than my father's. I turned, feeling that stupid relief rush back into my chest when Kiel walked into the room. "Mr. Carelli," he tried, lifting his hands in some semblance of surrender that kept my father quiet. "This has been such a bad situation, and I realized, after all this time..."

Papa threw the tumbler to the floor, the heavy glass shattering against the marble tile. Kiel pulled me back, keeping me clear of the shards of glass and scotch.

"You come here? To *my* house," Papa started, voice lethal, furious as he pointed at Kiel. "Disrespect *my* home when I don't want you here?"

"Papa, please..."

"No! *Basta*!" He motioned toward us, and on a few thundering feet, my father's men swept into the room, standing on either side of Kiel and me. "Go away. Now!" he shouted at us.

Papa wouldn't hear reason, not yet. Once my father was angry, once he'd felt betrayed, there would be no calming him. It was best to walk away and give him the space he needed.

I nodded, taking Johnny's hand when he reached for me, walking with both Kiel and me as the guards waited for us.

"*Figlio*," my father growled, and my brother stopped, standing in the center of the room. It was as if there was some tether Papa kept him on that prevented him from leaving with us. Vinnie had disappeared somewhere between my confession and my father's furious curses, and that, at least, made me breathe a little easier. Kiel led me down the hall with his palm in the center of my back. His gaze shifted around us as we navigated the hallways until we came to the front entrance and my black S-Class, door opened, my own guards waiting for me.

"Bella," I heard behind me. Vinnie pushed off the stucco next to the door. He didn't bother acknowledging Kiel. Instead, the man kept that ridiculous grin on his face. Only now it felt like half a threat, like Vinnie knew something good, something juicy that he was bursting to share with me. "Don't be stupid."

"Excuse me?" I lifted a hand when Kiel came to my side, looking ready to push me behind him just to keep Vinnie at a distance.

"You heard me fine, *puttana.*"

This time, Kiel *did* stand in front of me, glaring down at Vinnie, who was at least three inches shorter than him.

"You need to back the fuck up," he told Vinnie, seeming unworried by my father's guards as they moved away from the front door.

"Or what will you do, *figlio di puttana?*" Vinnie's mouth shifted then, and that condescending smirk became a grin that made my stomach twist. "You'll do nothing, and I will still laugh over your cold, dead body, *sì?*" He moved his jacket, flashing the black metal butt of his gun before he refastened the button. "You'll be dead, and I'll be fucking your wife in the ass while her papa hands me the keys to his business."

"Try me," Kiel said, seeming unworried by the guards or the weapon Vinnie had displayed. "Please, asshole, fucking try me." Kiel shook his head with a tight, lethal smile that scared me, that should have scared Vinnie if he had been smart enough to recognize the threat for what it was. But Vinnie stared at Kiel, unflinching, seemingly unworried. The seconds passed, the tension ratcheting up until Kiel gritted his teeth, his jaw clenching before he called over his shoulder to me, "Get in the car, Cara. *Now.*" His voice was deep, the tone another threat.

I decided not to challenge him. Vinnie was a disgusting asshole, but he also had a gun. I moved quickly, slipping into my Benz, muttering under my breath in Italian to one of my guards, "Don't let anything happen to my husband," before they slammed the door shut. I sat there on those leather seats, watching Kiel and Vinnie square off against each other.

I couldn't make out what they said, but I did notice Kiel's stance. How much larger he was. How he didn't flinch or display any twitches the way Vinnie did. The big Samoan wasn't scared.

At least, if he was, he didn't let it show. I held my breath until Vinnie turned and left, my father's guards following him. It was only after Kiel was standing out there on the driveway alone that he finally turned, nodding a thanks to my guard when he opened the door for him.

"Take us to my hotel," he told my driver. His jaw was still working like it took effort to keep his voice even.

"Are you okay?" I asked him, getting only a nod back in answer. His profile was sharp, the fine lines around his eyes and the long slope of his nose making him look fierce, dangerous. "Kiel," I said, wanting him to look at me.

When he didn't, a little throb of anger surfaced. It was irrational and stupid, but I was only trying to make sure he was okay. Still, the way his muscles tightened around his face, in his neck had me reminding myself how imposing, how grumpy Kiel could be when he was pissed off.

I tamped down my irritation and swallowed back my anger, trying to make my voice sound soft and grateful. "What you did today... I... Well...thanks."

He moved his head, taking most of that profile from me as he looked out the window. His jaw never relaxed. Kiel took a breath, his throat working as he exhaled. "The shit you got me in," he said, voice raspy, reminding me of a growl some feral animal might make before he pounced, "...it just got deeper."

Chapter Nine
Kiel

Cara had tells.

There were small things she did. Little tics that gave you a heads-up that something had pissed her off. Since I'd been back in New York, I'd half convinced myself she'd outgrown those small giveaways.

Maybe, I told myself, she'd managed to get her temper under wraps. Happens all the time. Time and distance had a way of maturing us all. We considered the stupid bullshit we got ourselves into, and later, with time and distance, we cringed at how senseless we'd been.

It wasn't until the car ride from her father's house that I realized how wrong I'd been. She'd asked, casually, what Vinnie had said to me. I wasn't going to repeat that shit.

Things were messy enough already.

No need to make it worse. When I ignored her question, Cara took it in stride, thanking me for the rescue, watching me as I glared blindly outside the window.

I'll fuck her, then I'll fuck her up, sì?

That hadn't been a vague threat. You didn't say shit like that to another man and not mean it. Vinnie was dangerous. Stupid, but still dangerous. He had clout and cash. It was likely the only reason Cara's old man wanted to join their families. I'd done enough stories on crime bosses and the dirty shit professional thugs did to each other to know when one of them was full of shit. Money gave you a false sense of security, but it also got you whatever the fuck you wanted. The look in Vinnie's eyes told me he wanted what Carelli had. He'd go about getting that any way he could.

That's what had occupied my thoughts as Cara went from thanking me for backing her up, to grunting under her breath when I didn't answer, to jerking her foot so hard the seat shook as we made it back into the city and to my hotel.

By the time she uttered one final, "What the hell did Vinnie say?" we'd cleared the lobby and made it to the elevator.

"Kiel..." She tried again, going quiet when I twisted my gaze toward her, my head moving in a slow, careful turn. My mouth pinched with a frown, eyes squinted tight, but not even my frown or the "shut the fuck up" look I gave her did anything to quash her temper.

By the time she stalked into the hotel room and spun around with her hands resting on those luscious hips, I knew her anger had crested and I was about to hear her yell.

"Tell me what he said to you. *Now*."

This time, there was no question. Nothing that got backed up with her gratitude.

This time, Cara yelled and didn't seem to give a shit how her loud mouth got under my skin.

The keycard bounced against the coffee table when I threw it and my cell down, turning on her to give back the icy glare she gave me. Cara had gotten used to barking orders, that was clear. God knew her men and her father's goons always jumped when she told them to, but I wasn't a fucking puppy.

If she barked at me, I'd damn sure bite back. "It's not important," I said, rubbing my face when she didn't kill the brimming temper tantrum.

I didn't need this shit—any of it.

Vinnie, her father, fucking Cara herself, and the drama that always followed her? I thought that part of my life was behind me after I washed my hands of the Carelli family for good.

She released a low noise, something that reminded me of a half-drowned cat not the least bit happy to be wet, and stomped forward, nostrils flaring. "Like fuck, it isn't." She slammed her palms against my chest, trying to intimidate me, but I didn't budge. "I have every—" she jabbed one long red fingernail into my chest "—right—" *jab* "—to—" *jab* "—know—" The jabbing stopped when I grabbed her fingers, but Cara continued, "—to know what that asshole said to you."

Her hand shook when I gripped her wrist, peeling her fingers away from my chest. It took two full inhales for me not to lash out.

This was us.

We did angry well.

If I weren't careful, we'd scream, curse, and push each other's limits. Then I'd end up with my dick deep inside her and her nails bloodying my back.

Couldn't let that happen, but fuck, was Cara beautiful when she was mad. Those big, lush lips curled and pouted. Her eyes got darker, gleamed against the dim light in the room, and a beautiful rush of pink brightened her face. So fucking beautiful and deadly. And also frustrating and the single most stubborn bitch in the world. The look she gave me when I pulled her hand from my chest got grittier somehow. It made her look unhinged. Touching her was dangerous when she was mad, and right now, the woman was livid. She seemed to expect me to cower and back away. Maybe she knew how she looked. Definitely knew how that look used to affect me. But I wasn't her brother or her old man. The pout, the glares, the loss of control did not work on me anymore.

Much.

Five years ago, I might have caved to her too. But she killed that version of me, showing her true colors and her ability to throw me...*us*...away.

"I'm not on your father's payroll." I tightened my fingers around her wrist, not letting her go as she struggled against my hold. "You don't get to bark orders at me."

"That's right," she seethed, still jerking at her hand like she had any hope of breaking free from my grip. "You're my *husband*." She practically spat the word in my face. Hurling the term at me like it was supposed to mean something. Fuck, just that word from her mouth had my own temper brimming.

When I managed to speak, my words came out through clenched teeth as I tried to stop myself from yelling in her face. "Only when it's convenient, *wife*." I shook my head, sure that my own anger and disgust at what she'd done to me were clear and present in my expression. "For five fucking years, I didn't exist to you. Now you want to pretend I meant any fucking thing? You used me like a dog, then ran from me like a fucking coward. I meant nothing to you."

Cara rocked back. A soft, barely audible gasp passed through her gaping mouth like my words were a punch to her gut. "How can you say that to me?"

"You threw me to the wolves without worrying about my feelings, or hell, even my life. Let's stop lying to each other. I was working a story, you were covering your ass." I dropped her hand, forcing a laugh when her eyes went wide. "The off-the-charts sex, though, that was just a perk of the job." Those words felt thick on my tongue and tasted bitter. God help me, I couldn't stop myself from hurting her. She'd done the same to me. She'd still do the same to me given half a chance.

Vinnie was a threat. Cara was an opportunist, and she'd pulled me back into the bullshit of her family life. For just a second, I wanted to hurt her. I wanted to give back a taste of the pain she'd given me.

"Fucking isn't enough. Never was. Bottom line of us, *sweetheart*? We had something small. Inconsequential and little thing that it was, you killed it. That shit will stay fucking dead, just like my feelings for you."

The sound Cara released then sounded more guttural. More primal than before. I expected her rage. I expected her fury, but I didn't expect her to clench her hand into a fist and lunge forward, coming at me like she wanted to see me bleed.

"Hell no," I said, grabbing one arm and twisting her. Cara's back thudded against my chest, and I pulled her against me tightly, holding her free arm out to the side.

"Let me go, Kiel," she said, clenching her jaw so tightly only her lips moved.

"Tell me you love me, then," I teased, baiting her into saying the words that used to slip from her mouth so easily. I brushed my lips against her jaw, sliding them so close to her mouth I could feel her warm breath blow across my face. "Tell me you want me, Cara."

She parted her lips as she slid her gaze to mine, finally stilling in my arms. "Fuck you."

"You always loved to, didn't you?" She growled as I moved my hand to her ass, cupping her cheek roughly and pressing her ass against my cock. "Doggy. Missionary. Head down, ass up. Reverse cowgirl." I smirked, basking in her anger, knowing my attitude was getting to her. But I wasn't a liar. Fuck, she loved to mix it up with me. *Reverse cowgirl.*

Her favorite and mine.

Hell, I still had fantasies about that shit.

"Kiel," she said, whispering my name like she used to when I'd slide between her thighs, teasing her until she begged for my cock.

Cara didn't budge when I dropped her free arm to tangle my fingers in all that thick, dark hair. I guided her head, twisting her face close to sweep my tongue across her bottom lip. I remembered the sweet taste only Cara had and teased myself in the process. "The way you'd rock into me, taking me deep, clawing at my back, and moaning my name."

Cara tilted her head until our lips touched. The anger was almost gone from her expression. Without realizing how it had happened, my cock twitched. The throb of it worsened when Cara rubbed her round ass against me.

I hated her.

I wanted her.

So much shit got tangled in my head over this woman, I didn't think I'd ever be able to free myself from her completely.

She licked her bottom lip, that warm muscle sliding against my mouth. Her breath was hot and slow and so fucking delicious. "Please," she whispered and squeezed her eyes closed.

I released her hair, turning her to slide my hand down her arm until I found the curve of her waist. Her breathing faltered, eyes still closed as I dragged my tongue across her lips and tasted her sweet mouth.

A small, low moan escaped the back of my throat as I tasted her warm mouth, remembering the way our bodies used to move together.

We'd been so in sync. So connected. It was a dance with no steps.

Just our bodies.

Just the moment and the deep, ancient need to touch and devour and *be*. "I've missed you." She moved her arm around my neck as I skated a hand up her ribs, coming to rest under her breasts with my thumb dangerously close to her nipple. Cara shuddered, pushing her breasts closer to my hand. "I've missed us."

My resistance was nearly nonexistent now. Cock hard. Head full of her scent. Her warm, fit body against me and that break in control only cracked wider when she tangled her fingers in my hair and pressed her lips to mine.

In that moment, I wasn't thinking about how much I'd loved her. There was only the sensation of what she did to my body. How easy it was to remember that dance again and claim this woman's body.

It wouldn't last. How could it?

I'd buried the hurt I'd never totally forgotten. But I still remembered every bit of pain, betrayal, and regret I'd felt since the day I left New York, cursing the day I ever let myself get wrapped up with Cara.

One last time, I told myself as I swept a thumb across her nipple, putting into motion something I knew I couldn't stop.

I wanted the end I didn't get five years ago.

I wanted one last touch that would really be the last.

I wanted her to beg.

"Say you want me," I growled as I kneaded her ass and my hard cock strained against my jeans, pleading to get lost in her one last time.

"I...I want you, Kiel." Her voice was sweet and soft as she said my name, the sound like a weak purr that took effort to release. Cara blinked slowly, gaze shifting around my face, tits moving closer to my touch, then she released one last moan, a hum that sounded like want and need and fucking sex itself. "I... Shit, *Kiel,*" she said, eyes half lidded but still hungry. "Fuck me," she moaned.

Any fight I had left died in that moment at those two moaned words.

Need overcame anger and hurt.

Hunger took betrayal.

The urge to touch her was overwhelming.

I found the bottom of her shirt, slowly gliding my fingers across her velvet skin as I lifted the top over her head, exposing her strapless black lace bra.

I leaned forward, dragging my tongue against the swell of her breasts. She tipped her head back, offering herself to me as she shoved her hands under my shirt. That touch seared me, those sharp nails against my ribs as she sank them into my skin, trembling against my arms. The pace was too slow, and it had been too long. Now need took precedence, and I slipped my fingers under her bra, pulling the fabric free and tossing it to the floor.

Cara went at me with the same desperate speed, fingers moving frantically, yanking at the button of my jeans and fumbling with my zipper as my mouth closed around one nipple while I pinched the other.

The tremble left her limbs as she slid her fingers into my waistband, forcing my pants down far enough for my cock to spring free. The warmth of her palm enveloped me, turning the dull ache into a deep, painful throb only she could soothe.

For a moment, I forgot I hated her.

In that split second, with my lips tightening around her nipple, her hand sliding against my cock, she owned me just like she had before she crushed my heart and tossed me out like a piece of trash.

This wasn't about loving each other.

That moment had passed, and our fucking had never been tender or sweet.

It wouldn't be now.

My cock was like solid rock in her expert hand as she stroked my shaft harder, faster, so tight and hot that I had to pull away.

I grabbed her shoulders, regretting the moment her hand slipped from my skin. I spun her around and bent her over the couch. She pushed her ass out, offering all she had, and I was more than happy to take everything I could.

I moved one hand from her cheek, using it to tug my shirt over my head and slid my free hand to her thighs, bunching her skirt near her waist before I rested my fingers between her legs. I wanted her warm flesh against me. I wanted everything she offered.

She gasped as my tongue caressed the curve of her ear and my fingers glided across her slick skin. "Always so wet for me, Cara." She started to rise, but I pressed my front against her back, ending the last bit of fight she had as my fingers slipped to her opening. "Tell me to stop, and I will."

I gave her one final out. One way to stop what was about to happen, but I knew she wouldn't.

We both wanted it.

We both craved the feel of the other's touch from the moment our bodies came together.

No amount of time or pain changed that.

She peered over her shoulder, panting as I pushed my fingertips through her wetness, teasing her. "More... Give me...more, and don't stop," she rasped with her chin in my hand, holding her head back so I could see her eyes.

I smiled against her ear, more than happy to give her what she wanted, hating and loving her at the same time. "Always a greedy little cunt," I told her as I pushed my fingers inside, filling her.

Cara thrust her ass backward, always eager, always taking without asking and having no remorse.

That was the thing about my wife I'd learned after my world fell apart. She felt no guilt. Felt no grief about her brother almost ending my life or sending the cops after me. Just as I felt no compassion or pity for the way I was about to fuck her, using her for pleasure and nothing more.

Rocking against her, I bit the delicate curve of her shoulder near her neck, plunging my fingers deeper. My cock glided across the soft skin of her ass, throbbing to be buried deep inside her. Cara's pussy clamped down on my fingers like she loved the way I stroked her.

That shit hadn't changed.

She was still so eager to show me how much she liked what I did to her body.

Cara's pants and low moans echoed in my ear as I licked across her skin, soothing the teeth marks I no doubt left.

So hot.

So sweet, so ready to be fucked.

I couldn't take it anymore.

I tugged my hand backward, placing the tip of my cock where my fingers had just been. She shifted, rocking forward on her tiptoes as I plunged my dick into her, impaling her until there was no more to take.

I wrapped my hand around her waist, holding her in place as I pummeled into her. Those low, hungry moans were like a song. Something fast like heavy metal, a machine-gun blast of music and sound, and fuck, did I love every note.

She writhed underneath me. Five thrusts in and she was already begging for more. Her fast, throbbing pulse beat against my fingers as I wrapped them around her neck, slipping my hand up to tangle her hair in my fist.

She screamed, "Oh God," as I tightened my grip, tipping her head back and controlling her movement.

But God wasn't going to save her or give her absolution.

Only me.

The man she'd wronged.

The one she claimed to love, but only when it was convenient.

I let out a growl, shoving my cock so deep even I lost my breath. The familiar tingle traveled up my spine as my muscles strained, chasing the orgasm I wanted more than air. My even strokes became stunted and unsteady as my balls grew heavy, slapping against her ass with each forward push. She rocked backward, sliding her hand between her legs to give herself the orgasm I wasn't going to give her.

The first upsurge of pleasure crashed over me, sending shock waves through my system as I shuddered against her back. I gasped, trying to find air but unable to breathe as I picked up the pace, riding the last crest and spilling everything I had into my wife.

Cara moaned, stroking her clit faster as she followed me down the spiral. Panting, I released her hair, pressing my body against her back, and she shuddered underneath me.

"Fuck," she whispered.

"We did," I told her, pushing away from her, wanting this over and done. There wouldn't be any cuddling or spooning as we drifted off to sleep.

Vinnie had worried me, but not enough that I'd be making bullshit professions of love.

Cara turned, body glistening with sweat and her skirt still bunched around her waist. "Kiel," she said, taking a step forward as I moved back.

I shook my head, not wanting to hear anything she had to say as I pulled up my pants. "Don't start."

She frowned, and I saw the swift flash of hurt that she tried to tamp down. It didn't work, and I ignored the nagging voice in my head that called me out for being an asshole. She opened her mouth but didn't speak, and I scrubbed my face, throwing a smirk on my mouth at the frown she gave me.

"It is what it is, sweetheart. Now it's over. You've got protection. Those goons of yours will have your back. Go home."

Her eyes flashed, a mix of anger and hurt crossing her face, and her hands balled into fists at her sides. "But we just..." She motioned between us, jerking a glare at me when I laughed.

She watched me as I tucked my cock away and zipped my pants. "I never wanted to be mixed up in your father's business, but you pulled me in without giving two fucks about my life or what I wanted."

Cara took a step. An excuse was ready on her tongue from the way she immediately opened her mouth, but I shook my head, stopping her bullshit before she could speak it. "You want a husband, and I want that newspaper gig. You need protection, fine. I'll give it to you. But don't expect much more than that from me."

"But we..." she repeated, like she couldn't believe I'd fuck her and not want more. "You just..." Moisture pooled in her eyes, and her lip trembled as I grabbed my shirt off the floor. Her voice was soft as she placed her hand over her mouth. "You can't expect me to believe you feel nothing for me at all."

"I never said I didn't. If something happens to you, it would piss me off. Something bad happens to you, maybe I'd get shit square with whoever did that to you." I pulled the shirt over my head, not caring that it was wrinkled and smelled like sex. "But that doesn't mean I'm a gullible asshole willing to dive right back between your thighs anytime you want to fuck me."

When Cara flinched, as though my words punched her in the gut, I tilted my head, honestly confused why she looked so damn hurt. "What?" I asked, raising an eyebrow.

"I thought..."

"I took what I wanted just like you always do. I fucked you, nothing more."

She lurched forward, hand in the air, ready to strike again, but I grabbed her arm, stopping her. "I hate you," she said, her voice low, icy, and full of venom.

"That makes two of us."

But I wasn't talking about Cara.

God, I loved her.

Even now with her eyes shining, lips pulled tight, baring her teeth, I wanted her.

She deserved the panic, the unsettled feeling deep in her stomach, the pain of being abandoned.

For five years, I'd tried to convince myself I hated her. The person I hated the most in the world was myself.

I hated that I loved her.

I hated that I cared.

I hated that I wasn't sure I could turn my back and walk away even if I wanted her to think I could.

Chapter Ten
Cara

There were never enough choices.

Money and power could bring you a few.

They did their part to open doors and keep those bastards from closing again, but that didn't go very far.

It didn't make someone love you.

Or, in my case, love you again.

My husband fucked me like a whore. Bent me over a sofa and took what he wanted.

Normally, I wouldn't have complained; every way Kiel touched me shot fire and need through my veins. But he'd touched me two nights ago and promised it meant nothing.

I meant nothing.

The fuck did you expect?

I'd been a coward. I'd left him to my brother and the assholes that did my father's bidding. Kiel wasn't wrong. I'd treated him as a husband of convenience.

Like he was nobody.

I fucked you, nothing more.

That admission went deep.

It reminded me of what I'd done five years ago.

It reminded me of the pain I'd caused him.

Now Kiel was giving it all back to me.

Has your husband called yet?

I thought of not responding to my brother's text. He'd been in on this plan from the beginning, from the second I'd told him the truth about Kiel and me. Now he was concerned, but that had nothing to do with my marriage and everything to do with how hurt my father had been.

No.

My thumb hovered over the phone as I hesitated with what I wanted to know. I was proud. I was stubborn, but I was still worried about my father.

Is Papa still angry?

The small dots on the message flitted across the screen, and I was sure Johnny was writing a paragraph. Maybe I hoped he was, but when he stopped typing and the text came through, I guessed my brother had written, erased, and rewritten the truth repeatedly. Each one would likely sting less than the one before.

He's at least stopped calling you THAT GIRL.

I lowered my shoulders, dropping into my desk chair with my phone between my fingers as I typed.

Nice. That gives me so much hope. Thanks.

Johnny returned a quick *What did you expect?* followed by a quicker *It'll all work out* before I threw my phone onto the desk, reclining a little in my padded leather office chair.

"Ms. Carelli?" my assistant, Sarah, called through the phone, her voice clipped but professional.

"Yes?" I answered.

"You wanted me to remind you of the new inventory at the FH. You said you'd take a look during your lunch, and it's almost one."

"Thanks, Sarah. I'll be a couple of hours."

It would take me at least fifteen minutes with lunch hour traffic. I wasn't in a hurry to get to the gallery or see the obnoxious snob who ran the place.

Carelli money was old.

It was vast, but to some of New York's elite, like Mitsi Wallace-Carmichael, Finnegan Holden's curator, it was still not worthy.

We were thugs, plain and simple. It didn't matter that we hosted multimillion-dollar fund raisers and charitable galas. Didn't matter one lick to her that we'd discovered three MacArthur Fellows. To her, to the people like her, we were criminals throwing money around to win respectability.

We were.

That was the whole damn point of my job at the museum. Legitimacy. And I did my best to earn it.

For the most part, we had. But there were still people like Mitsi who never saw beyond the gossip that swirled around our name.

I pulled on my coat, buttoning it as I left my office, intent on wearing it and the bullshit gossip I knew was thick in the air like a cape.

Let them talk.

Page Six, I was sure, had a lot to say about Vinnie and me. We were seen together once, a month or so ago, and we'd been followed ever since. Even more aggressively because Vinnie hadn't hidden his long-term girlfriend from the paparazzi. If the news broke that whatever was happening between us was off because I was already married, the attention we'd get would be relentless. Especially if they put two and two together and linked Kiel with his famous brother and the cable show he co-hosted with his equally famous girlfriend, Kit Carlyle.

Arturo, my driver, waited at the front of the museum, ready to hold open the door for me as I moved toward the lobby. At least it was him and not the other guards my father insisted I hire. With Arturo there waiting for me and my father's anger still thick and raging, I'd figured Dante and Giovanni wouldn't be necessary. They'd just scare patrons from coming inside the museum.

Arturo, though, was a professional, less intimidating than my guards, and it was his plain, dispassionate face I focused on as I walked toward him. He had to be pushing fifty and looked like some exaggerated cartoon version of what a mafia goon would look like—no neck, too-wide shoulders, jaw cut into lines and sharp edges. The thought made my top lip quirk, but I pressed my mouth tight and focused on the rich smell of cinnamon wafting through the rooms as Beth, the front desk receptionist, sipped on the white hot chocolate she seemed to think she successfully hid from me behind her desk.

Kiel had loved cinnamon in his hot chocolate, and I'd never been able to fight back the memory of him sprinkling the spice into his cup as we huddled together waiting for a cab that would take us from NYU and back to my apartment on the Upper West Side.

He'd wrap his massive arm around me, pulling me against his chest as we shared the cocoa, and that sweet spice would move into my sinuses. "This is good, right? Making our own heat?" he'd joked, kissing my forehead when I'd nodded a reply.

We made our own heat, always.

We had two nights ago in his hotel room.

"Signora," Arturo greeted, opening the door for me, and I hurried through it, trying to push away the memory of that frigid winter afternoon and Kiel's warm body. I didn't need to be reminded of what he

felt like when he took me. Not then, not two nights ago either. It was pointless. Especially now that I'd been relegated to a body he'd used.

I took what I wanted just like you always do.

The car was parked twenty feet from the front of the museum, and I cleared my throat, wishing the knot in it would vanish. It hadn't left me since I'd hightailed it away from Kiel's hotel. My body aching, my heart a shredded mess as I sank down in the back seat of my car, letting the tears collect on my lashes before I wiped them away.

Damn Kiel for making me feel this guilt.

Damn him for reminding me I was nothing to him and wouldn't ever be again.

Hand on the open car door, I tossed in my bag and was about to slide inside when I heard my name being called in a deep and kind tone behind me. I exhaled, eyes squinted tight, wanting half a second to rein in my anger and embarrassment before I turned to face him.

"If you're curious about the job," I started, figuring the position I'd promised him was the only reason Kiel would bother to track me down. "I told you, Raquel is still interested."

"That's not why I'm here," Kiel said, glancing at Arturo when the driver stepped in front of me.

"It's fine," I told my guard before I tapped his arm to move him back. "Kiel's wounds are always inflicted in private."

Kiel jerked his gaze from Arturo's face to mine at my small dig. I repressed the instant urge to roll my eyes at him when he gritted his teeth, jaw moving like he needed to remind himself not to yell. If he was insulted, he kept it to himself.

"I need to say something to you," he told me, his features tightening when I only stared back at him. Kiel stepped forward, taking one hand out of his jacket to rest his palm on the open door at my side. "Please."

He wasn't a man who liked to wait. Before, when we were together, he'd been gentler. Kinder. He'd been worried about my opinions, my thoughts, and he always wanted me happy. But Kiel had never liked waiting for anything. The things he wanted, he wanted instantly, and by the way he gripped the door and narrowed his black eyes, it told me that hadn't changed much.

When he moved another step closer and Arturo followed him, I shot a glance between the two men, figuring it would be bad for business to have Kiel and my driver tussling outside the museum.

"Fine," I said finally, nodding to the driver so he'd step back. "I have to go to the FH—"

"The FH?"

"Yes. The Finnegan Holden Gallery." Kiel gave me a blank stare, reminding me of a kid trying to sort out a complicated geometry problem, and I shook my head, turning to slide into the car. "Follow or don't. Either way, I need to be there."

The interior was warm, but my fingers were still cold since I'd forgotten my gloves at my place. I took to rubbing my hands together, blowing hot air into my palms as Kiel climbed inside next to me.

He looked at my face, then down at my cupped hands before he sighed, stretching a gloved hand toward me to pull my fingers between his massive palms. "You always forget your gloves," he said, rubbing our fingers together, trying to generate some heat.

"I was in a hurry."

"Takes literally three minutes to tug them on and get out of your place." His hot breath tickled my cold skin when he blew across my knuckles, his attention on me and whatever expression was trapped on my face. Kiel shook his head, keeping whatever he thought to himself. "You still keep your gloves in that entry table of your grandmother's?" I nodded but didn't speak. "You still run at least five minutes late every day?" Another nod and Kiel smiled, but the grin left his mouth almost as soon as it got there. "Keep your cell in the same table so you won't forget."

He finished his little doling out of Kiel wisdom, but he didn't look away from me. Did he want more of the same treatment we'd given each other that night in his hotel, or was this visit meant to serve a specific purpose? When Kiel went on watching me, his hot breath moving over my cold fingers, I extracted them, returning his heavy stare.

"I'm good," I told him, folding my arms over my chest. I didn't want the temptation of touching him to be so accessible. "Now, what do you want?"

The warm smirk that had moved his lips left his mouth completely, and Kiel leaned back, resting his hands in his lap as he watched me again. He looked good today in a charcoal gray pea coat and thick black scarf with no frills or embellishments. He wasn't a man who went in for glitz in his wardrobe. He always dressed well, but he dressed like a man with no intention of impressing anyone.

It annoyed me that he looked so damn good. Especially after he'd promised I was nothing to him.

"The other night..." he started, voice like liquid fire, as though just the reminder of it did something to his body that he tried and failed to control. "It was..."

"Insulting," I offered, grinning to myself when Kiel's nostrils flared.

"No," he asserted, not holding back the smile now. "It was fierce, hot, and fucking incredible, but then, it always is when I'm inside you, Cara."

"It..." I tried again, staring out the window as Arturo moved us through the city. "*It* was good. You, on the other hand, were insulting."

"Hmm," Kiel mused, resting against the seat, his focus on my face. I swore I could feel him watching me, like he wanted to soak up every ounce of my skin.

"Does any of that matter?" I asked, focusing on the traffic Arturo weaved through with ease as I unfolded my arms and tried to relax. The streets weren't nearly as busy as I'd suspected they would be, and my driver took advantage.

"Any of what?"

His scent was thick, rich, some obscure cologne I couldn't place. From the look and smell of him, Kiel had done a little shopping. No way that coat or the tailored suit I spotted underneath could have been stuffed in the duffle he'd had with him at the airport. My mouth watered, my senses overloaded in just the few minutes we'd been together in the car.

"You and me and whatever fierce 'fucking incredible' thing that happened." My hand was on the seat between us, and I curled my fingers into a ball when Kiel brushed my palm. "I...mean nothing," I told him, gradually turning to watch the slow, careful way he brushed the skin of my wrist.

"That's what brought me here." His admission came out slowly. Like a whisper he wanted only me to hear. I frowned, watching him move closer. When I didn't respond, gave him only a look, my eyes narrowed and nothing more, Kiel sighed, the bottom lid of his right eye twitching. "What, Cara?"

"You're full of shit."

"Why do you say that?"

"Two nights ago, I was treated like a whore." My voice was loud, biting. I spotted the swift movement of Kiel's gaze to Arturo and back again to my face. Was he embarrassed that I spoke so freely? "You bent me over your sofa and fucked me hard while I fingered my clit. It was hot. Fierce, like you said, and not two minutes after you fucked me, you told me I was nothing. So, yeah. You're full of shit." I turned, head tilted as I watched him, curious why he looked so uneasy.

Then something occurred to me.

Something that seemed so familiar because it was motivation I used myself. Kiel wasn't smiling. He didn't do anything but watch how I twisted on the seat, hands back in my lap as I shot my eyebrows up, taken aback that he'd stoop to my very obvious level. "Uh-huh, full of shit or you want something."

Kiel controlled his features, keeping his expression even. Not daring to give away even the smallest emotion for nearly an entire minute. The look was stern, a little infuriated, but I didn't back down. I only blinked twice, less than he had, and kept my composure as well. Finally, with his mouth twitching and that lower lid still pulsing, Kiel leaned back, elbow on the door, finger at his temple as he shook his head.

"My brother doesn't like you," he told me.

"Ah. Okay. That makes everything so clear, *stronzo*."

He held up a hand, keeping me silent as he continued. "I went back to Seattle busted and bruised, a fact that I've repeated several times since I've been in the city, *I know*. No need for the eye roll." He released a breathy grunt when I made a face, then he dismissed my attitude with a headshake.

"And that has what to do with your brother not..." I frowned then, realizing at least some of what he meant. Of course, Kane Kaino didn't like me. It was my fault his kid brother had landed back home injured and hurt. I looked down, fiddling with the hem of my skirt while he waited for me to continue. "Fine. He hates me."

"I never said he hates you. I said he doesn't like you."

"There's a difference?"

The small noise he released must have been a laugh. It at least came with a grin. A dangerous-looking smirk I couldn't decide whether should turn me on or make me worry. Then Kiel's smile deepened, just one dimple denting his right cheek.

"You'd know if a Kaino really hated you. Trust me." His features relaxed. The sharp edge of his jaw didn't make him seem fierce or intimidating when he smiled like that. For just a second, no more than a half-held breath that lodged in my chest, Kiel looked like that easygoing, sweet kid I'd fallen for five years ago.

"He didn't want me coming here because he figured you weren't done with me. He's rarely wrong." His large shoulder moved with his shrug, and Kiel glanced out the window as though he didn't want to see my reaction when he admitted what had changed his attitude. "So last night when he called, I filled him in."

"Let me guess, he still doesn't like me?"

"Couldn't say." He moved his head toward me, shifting one glance at my face before his attention went back to the street and the slow journey we made toward Fifth Avenue. "Kane is so wrapped up in his feelings for Kit, there isn't much drama that can get under his skin." One last scan of the sidewalk then Kiel gave me his attention again. "He gave me the usual advice. 'Watch your back. Don't trust anyone.' Shit I knew, but then he asked if I'd fucked you." Kiel's mouth twitched when I shot my eyebrows up. "I admitted I had, and he gave me the heavy, disappointed sigh. But when I told him you meant nothing, that I'd *told* you as much, that sigh got kinda growly, and my brother yelled at me for twenty minutes."

The door handle bit into my back when I shifted against it, looking up into the bemused expression that shifted the tension from Kiel's face. "Because you insulted a woman he doesn't like?"

"Because I used you. Because...I *lied* to you." Kiel dropped his voice and scooted closer, elbows on his knees, his careful cool slipping a fraction. "Kane doesn't like liars. He especially doesn't like liars who use those lies to get what they want."

"And you wanted...?"

It was three long seconds before he spoke. Three thousand milliseconds of Kiel watching me, looking like he wasn't sure how much of an apology I deserved. Then he pressed his palms into his eyes, and the twitching lid stopped. "I wanted you. I'm not such a bastard that I won't admit that."

"But—"

He interrupted me with a slow headshake, and he stretched his hand out to mine. "No buts. No howevers. No caveats. My brother reminded me that I'm not a liar. We aren't wired that way. When I say something, I generally meant it. Kane does too, but that night in my room, I was so pissed off about the entire situation—your father, Vinnie's threats, and being thrown in the mix again that I..." He inhaled, threading our fingers together as though he needed my touch to give him strength. "I just wanted to be away from it all. I was pissed that I couldn't be. More than that, I was pissed I couldn't stop wanting you."

"Wanting someone who means..."

"I told you," he started, tightening his grip against my fingers. "I lied. I don't want this life. The violence. The mafia bullshit. Not any of it. But I can't lie to you anymore, Cara. I hate what you did to me. I hate how badly you hurt me. I hate that you manipulated me to get me back into your life." He turned, tugging on my hand until it rested against his thigh. "But I don't hate you."

"You took me even when you didn't—"

"I'll *never* stop wanting you. No matter what you do. There will always be something between us." Kiel lifted my knuckles to his chest, holding my hand there as he rubbed his thumb over my skin. "Call it heat. Call it need. I don't care, but I want you. That won't stop. I may not like it, but there's the truth of it all." Jaw tightening as he watched me, Kiel lowered my hand, replacing it on his knee but not holding it anymore. "I want to hate you, but I don't. I want to *not* want you, but I can't. Fucking pathetic, but that's my truth."

It took a lot for Kiel to admit the truth.

I had hurt him.

I had betrayed him worse than anyone else in his life.

He wasn't a man who took his licks in stride.

He always wanted retribution.

He wanted his enemies to know he never forgot.

In a lot of ways, he was like me.

Like my family.

Once a wrong had been done to us, it was kept locked tight in a vault of thick memory, never to be dismissed. Never to be pardoned.

Maybe that's what had drawn Kiel to me.

Maybe it was the same need for justice I saw in him that set us in each other's orbits.

But Kiel also had a heart. He understood.

If you wounded him, he wanted to know why.

Then he'd get his justice if you deserved it.

I did.

I knew I did.

This reversal of his feelings from two nights ago made my chest tighten.

It gave me hope that one day he could forgive me.

Still, not for nothing, I *was* a Carelli and, technically, also a Kaino. I'd let him pretend with the peace he offered, but I wasn't going to forget.

I knew he wouldn't either.

"So," I started, head to the side, eyes downcast to watch how close he'd put my hand to his thigh. "What do we do about this?"

Kiel smiled, a small glimmer of pleasure glinting in his eyes as he watched me. "Well, I'm not gonna kick you out of my bed if the opportunity comes around again, but I'm also not going to treat you like a whore." He stretched an arm along the back of the seat and fingered my hair absently. "Not unless you ask."

"I won't."

The stroking of my hair stopped. Kiel pushed an exaggerated grimace onto his face as though he were disappointed and surprised by my reaction. "No whore treatment?"

"No sex." The grimace got real then, but I ignored it. "With us. Not again."

Kiel scratched his ear, pulling on it as though he needed a distraction to organize his thoughts. It was less than two seconds before that cool calm resurfaced, right along with a smooth grin and a flippant shrug. "That's disappointing, but I understand. I'm sorry I said you meant nothing. You might be manipulative and greedy for my attention, but you aren't meaningless to me. You never have been."

"Because you care if something bad happens to me?" I asked, remembering the only decent thing he'd said to me two nights ago.

"Because, Cara, against my wishes, you're my wife for however much longer that needs to be our reality. I might not like you most days, but God help me, you're still family." The smile vanished from his features. Kiel leaned close just as the car slowed next to the sidewalk in front of the gallery. There was something I recognized in his eyes—a steely glint that reminded me of the promises Kiel had made once. They'd been solid and real, and he'd meant every word. He reached for my face, brushing away a strand from my cheek like it was his right. Like five years hadn't separated him from the last time he'd touched me with such sweetness.

"Kainos protect family. Even when they don't deserve it."

I held his hand next to my face when he started to pull away, keeping that large palm against my skin. "Think I'll ever deserve it again?"

He bit at the inside of his lip, cautious, wary, before he answered. "Maybe. Think you'll ever forgive me for treating you like a whore?"

"Maybe," I admitted, missing his hand when he dropped it into his lap. My cheek still felt warm. "But it might take something monumental to earn my forgiveness," I joked, laughing under my breath.

"Noted."

Arturo stood at Kiel's door, ready for the tap on the window telling him to let us out. I nodded toward the man, eager to get Kiel's attention on something other than our proximity or the heat currently humming between us as my driver stood outside in the crisp fall weather.

Kiel returned my nod, grinned back, and tapped a knuckle against the glass, easing out of the car and offering a hand to me once he stood. It was easy taking it, getting back into the ebb and flow of our actions— him opening doors for me or guiding me through a room with his large hand at the small of my back.

He was a gentleman, no matter what had happened between us. It seemed that hadn't changed about him. He went as far as shutting the door behind us, tucking my hand into the crook of his elbow as we walked a good forty feet from the car. He threw me a glance and a half smile, before his body went rigid and he and Arturo both stood perfectly still.

The sidewalks were almost empty. There were custodians from the gallery near the front garden, trimming away dead weeds and collecting small bits of trash. The guards around the entrance weren't paying attention to us, and two beat cops strolled west toward Sixth Avenue.

It seemed quiet, sure, but not unusual. Not with the weather turning cooler and the lunch hour crowd dwindling, but Kiel and Arturo shared a look I'd seen before when my father's guards were on edge.

A look that said there was a threat looming, and their senses and instincts had them on high alert. Kiel had never been anything more than a journalist, but if your beat put you in a world were violence and danger were commonplace, then you learned to listen to your gut. You learned to keep your defenses up and do battle when the shit gets thick.

By the look on Kiel's face, shit was thickening quickly.

"On the left," Arturo said, his accent heavy and laced with fear.

"At my back," Kiel said, voice no louder than a growl.

Then the world twisted.

Spun on its axis.

Sped up and slowed down all at the same time.

So much of what happened became a blur; something I tried to remember later but failed at organizing the details into anything other than flashes.

Kiel's growl had just left his mouth when one of the garden workers stood up straight, whistled a quick, sharp chirp of sound, then ran toward us.

Arturo grabbed his gun, drawing it with a speed that should not have been possible for someone with such a low center of gravity. Kiel pulled me against his chest, his thick arms over my shoulders and his large hand over my head as he half carried, half pulled me toward the car.

"Fuck!" he said when Arturo dropped next to the car after a shower of pops and bangs I recognized as gunfire.

There could have been dozens of goons coming for us. There could have been two. I couldn't see past Kiel's huge body and the cold sidewalk against my chest when he shoved me to the ground.

"Fuck!" he screamed again, lying on top of me while he tugged on Arturo's collar, pulling the driver toward us.

Blood flowed in a thick stream as the man struggled toward us. He was conscious, but he looked weak, barely able to do more than pass his gun to Kiel just as the gardener came close.

"Oddio!" the driver said, holding up his hands, curses heavy, angry as the attacker approached.

Kiel grabbed the gun, rolled onto his back, and squeezed off three rounds. "In the car, right fucking now," Kiel said, but I wasn't sure who he expected to listen to him.

My body shook, and I couldn't make my fingers move correctly. The door handle was too slick, the action to pull it too complicated especially when Arturo struggled, crawling on an elbow to open the door. "Cara, move!" Kiel shouted, tugging me up with one hand and stuffing Arturo into the front seat with the other.

There was so much blood on the beige leather in my car, and my driver wheezed and coughed as he leaned against the headrest. *"Padre nostro, che sei nei cieli, sia santificato il tuo nome,"* he started, and tears burned and blinded my eyes as I recognized the Our Father whispering in a rush from his mouth.

"Arturo, don't..." I tried, surprised my voice sounded frantic. "I won't allow you to start preparing for things that aren't coming!" I glanced around us on the street, willing Kiel to hurry to the other side of the car and get in the driver's seat. As a distraction, I pulled a handkerchief from my bag, holding it tight over the gunshot right at Arturo's collarbone.

"Padre nostro, che sei nei cieli," he started again, and I could only join him, figuring it couldn't hurt to ask for a little help.

It felt like an hour and half a second and a thousand years since we'd stepped out of the car and into an ambush.

Logically, I knew it was no time at all, and I exhaled the breath I'd been holding when Kiel finally jumped into the driver's seat, grabbed the key from Arturo's outstretched hand, and tore down Fifth Avenue.

"Are you hit?" he asked me, voice panicked as he glanced at my driver then back to me. "I can't stop to check, Cara. You have to tell me. Check yourself out..."

"I'm...fine," I said, head shaking when he reached an arm back toward me, grabbing my leg like he needed to touch me to see if I was still warm and alive and not bleeding to death on the sidewalk.

"Get your phone. Call Johnny. Put it on speaker." He bypassed two cabs as they tried blocking his attempt to merge. I closed my eyes, not wanting to see if anyone had gotten in his way. "Cara..."

"I don't know where..." The weak response came out in a sob, and my entire body shook.

"Check your bag. Do it now, baby." His grip turned viselike on my legs, and I used my free arm to dig through my bag, emptying it onto the seat. My phone was at the bottom, and I grabbed it, thumbing through my recent texts, Arturo's blood smearing over the screen.

"Yeah?" My brother answered after two rings, his voice quiet but amused.

"Carelli, this is Kiel," he said as I held the phone up. "We got hit."

"*Madonn'!*" The amused tone was replaced by breathy panic as Johnny moved. The sound of his feet pounding came through the receiver same as his cursing and shouted oaths and demands as he moved. "Cara?"

"I'm here, *ciccio*. I'm fine... I just..." My voice was weak, terrified-sounding, I was sure. I held on to Kiel's fingers as he gripped my knee.

"*Cazzo,*" Johnny answered, his voice cracking and his breath panting now. "Where are you? *Oddio,* you tell me now."

"You still got a plane for the museum?" Kiel asked, glancing from the street in front of him to the rearview. There were sirens in the distance, but no one followed us.

"We do."

"Meet me at the airport."

"Where are you taking my sister?" My brother had stopped running, and the loud rev of a car accelerating muffled his question.

Kiel glanced at me in the mirror, his eyes wide but fierce.

He looked determined.

He looked in control, and with that one look, I knew he would protect me.

Damaged marriage or not.

Betrayal or not.

Kiel would protect me.

He tightened his hand on the steering wheel and pushed down on the gas, answering my brother's question as though it was an afterthought. "I'm taking her to the only place that's safe right now."

Chapter Eleven
Kiel

Gangsters weren't stupid.

They'd be shitty at their jobs if they were.

Vinnie, and I'd bet my left nut that that asshole was responsible for the attack on us, wasn't a stupid gangster either.

We couldn't just book a hotel and hide out in Seattle until shit got sorted.

Money bought power.

Power created control, and that bastard had a lot.

Much as I hated it, we'd have to hide.

That took effort.

There was no quick escape or quicker exit once we landed.

Seattle was a city.

It had space and people. A clutter of distractions that would make us vulnerable. But Seattle wasn't where we needed to be. To get to *that* place, it would take time and a hike I wasn't sure Cara was up to.

"You're kidding, yeah?"

"Nope."

The jeans were her size, I knew that. No one knew that ass like I did. While I hadn't seen much of it in the past five years, I'd recently gotten reacquainted. The hips were still wide, the ass plump and perfect.

Size eight, easy. The boots, though...

"You can't expect me to trek up a mountain..."

She shut up when I yanked the hiking boots out of her hands, frowning at her attitude. The princess was resurfacing, and that asshole was pissing me off.

"You think that bullshit back in New York was a joke?" She shook her head and dropped the boots onto the floor of the truck Kane had left for me at the airport because the paparazzi was still breathing down his neck.

I grabbed her wrist, waving her own fingers at her. The tips were still stained with Arturo's blood despite the half hour Cara had spent in the airplane bathroom.

"This isn't from finger painting. These motherfuckers want me dead, and they don't seem to care in the least if you get mixed up in that shit." She blinked at me, and I pushed back the quick urge that came over me to touch her.

It was her fault, all of this. If scaring her got her dressed and up the mountain faster, I'd do it.

"Either get dressed, put on the damn boots, and follow me, or you can stay here and let Vinnie and his assholes bring you back to your father's. I'm sure that'll be fun for you."

"I didn't mean..."

"Doesn't matter what you meant, Cara." I tugged on the sweatshirt my brother had left for me in the cab of the truck and didn't look at her. "Just hurry the hell up."

The truck was older. Probably an early eighties Ford that I bet Kane had borrowed from someone on his crew. It got us from the airport and to the dirt road that hid our family's generous cabin. No trucks. No cars. Nothing but your feet and a little effort hauling up any supplies you'd need and you'd be there.

Kane and I had bought it ten years ago. Our mother's anxiety had worsened living in the city, and she wanted quiet, woods, and enough stars overhead that wouldn't be lost in the chaos around her in Seattle. She couldn't handle the hike, so Kane kept several ATVs chained and covered in a small shed near the bottom of the trail where a large, flat ridge had been cleared. The ATVs were gone. All up at the cabin, waiting for me to call for a ride, but I thought the princess could use the wilderness, and I'd feel better after the long walk.

Cara dressed in silence while I pulled on my boots and grabbed the backpack from the bed of the truck. Kane had outfitted it with plenty of supplies—flashlights and batteries, water bottles, and a compass watch with GPS altimeter, barometer, and thermometer that glowed yellow in the dimming light. There was also a burner phone, a handful of protein bars, and a first aid kit.

Maybe it was a little overkill, but Kane liked to be prepared. He liked me to be prepared too, but I could never quite get up to his level with that shit. My brother had also left me his Glock and a box of ammo. Wasn't sure if that was meant for shooting any animals that got in our way or the animals who'd already tried to kill us, but there wasn't time to think about it. He also left me, if the two pickups were any indication, some backup. Kane's own Ford and Dale's Chevy were parked next to my truck on the ridge across a small grouping of trees that hid the ATV shed. That asshole had my back, and apparently, so did his friend.

"The coat's a little big," Cara admitted, coming around to the back of the truck where I'd pulled down the tailgate. She glanced up at the sky, then tilted her head toward the trail that started on the other side of the ridge where I'd parked the old truck. "It'll be dark soon."

I knew that. I did have eyes. "That happens every night."

"Well, I just mean, how are we going to manage... in the dark?"

"A few hours in the dark won't kill you," I snapped, tucking the gun in my waistband before I slid on the backpack. My voice was sharp, and when Cara glanced at me, exhaling a long breath, I realized my attitude wasn't needed.

Hadn't I apologized to her this morning? Hadn't I promised I'd never treat her like I had the other night in my hotel room? Now I was biting her head off for asking questions.

Sensible questions that anyone born and raised in the city might have when faced with worn jeans, hiking boots, and a climb up mountainous terrain.

Pushing back my irritation, I stood in front of her, adjusting the lining on her coat and refastening the buttons so it fit more snugly around her small waist. "It'll get cold quick, but moving will keep us warm."

She nodded but didn't speak, going still as I pulled up her hood and slipped a small flashlight in her front pocket. When I made to pull away, Cara stopped me with her gloved fingers around my wrist. "I wasn't trying to be a brat," she admitted, moving her gaze up to look me square in the eyes. "I...I've never been in a situation like this, and I gotta admit...I'm out of my element." Cara nodded around us, to the trees and darkening sky, then she jerked her eyes at the noise of what sounded like an owl hooting above us.

"Nature?" I said, not keeping the laugh out of my voice. "I know damn well this isn't your element."

"Yeah, well, I'm more of an urban jungle woman." She squeezed my hand, attention again flying around and above us. "You sure you know how to get us to this cabin?"

"I could do that blindfolded."

"Yeah," she started, pulling the flashlight from her pocket as she followed me to the trail. "Let's not do the whole blindfolded hiking thing."

She was winded quickly, something that boggled my mind. "Drink slower," I told her, handing her another water bottle. Her small panting had me stopping ten minutes away from reaching the cabin. "You'll get sick if you down it too fast." She ignored me, taking long gulps like she hadn't had water in a month. My low laughter caught her attention, and Cara held the bottle near her mouth, holding it still as she glared at me.

"What?" she asked, the word breathy.

"I've seen you tackle ten blocks in four-inch boots, carrying a heavy Chanel bag over your shoulder and a large Triple Mocha Frappuccino in your hand, and not break stride. But this?" I waved my own bottle around us as we sat near the edge of the trail catching our breaths. "*This* has you all out of breath?"

Cara kicked me with the tip of her boot, and I laughed harder, earning a middle finger from my wife.

"Hello, it's up a mountain in the cold. Not remotely the same terrain as the Upper West Side." She slumped, shoulders lowering as she messed with the label on the water bottle. "Besides, I'm never...scared in New York."

Something happened to her expression then. Something that had me dropping any humor I still felt at her ridiculous shallow breaths. We'd put the mountain and miles between us and the shooting, a trek that did the job of distracting us, but that didn't mean in moments like this Cara wasn't still messed up a little by what had gone down.

She didn't say anything as I slipped next to her, forgetting the backpack and water bottle to pull her against me with one arm over her shoulder. "Don't be scared, Little Goddess. I've got you."

"You say that, but what if..." She went quiet again, head shaking. I did what I always did when Cara was nervous or worried or so frustrated she couldn't see straight. "Kiel..." she started, then shut up completely when I lowered my mouth to hers and kept her head still with one palm against her cheek.

Cara had promised she didn't want to sleep with me. She'd sworn this morning that she'd never ask to be in my bed again. But the way she kissed me back, the slow, deep push of her tongue against mine, how she arched toward me, taking as much as I gave, told a different story. I wanted to kiss her to keep her calm. I wanted my mouth and breath to ease away the worry that had morphed into dread and fear. Maybe it worked. Maybe it backfired. I only knew that if I went on kissing her, if she kept kissing me back like she was, then our trek up the mountain would go even slower.

It hurt like hell to back away from the sweet taste of her, but I manned up and did the right thing.

"Kiel..."

"Goddess..."

"Fuck's sake, I think I might puke." I heard, jumping to my feet when the voice shot out from the trail then traveled closer. My brother was an asshole. If I didn't know it from past experience, I'd get the impression from that smirk on his face, the same one cracking over his friend Dale's stupid mug too.

"The fuck are you doing?" I asked, relaxing the grip I had on the Glock at my waistband when those two assholes came nearer.

"Escorting you," Dale offered, still grinning. He at least kept his attention around us and not on me or Cara like my brother.

"You took too damn long," Kane said, standing in front of me long enough to nod and slap my shoulder. "Figured you were close, though." He turned his phone, grinning at the green and white tracking app with my number and "Little Asshole" for my name at the bottom of the screen. Asshole was tracking me the whole time. When I only glared at him, Kane laughed, stuffing his phone into his back pocket. "Come on. Stop making out with your woman, and let's get up to the cabin. Kit's made enough food for an army."

Kane didn't wait for me to ask a bunch of dumb questions, like *What the hell are you doing here?* or *Why the hell are Dale and Kit with you?* Instead, my brother nodded at my backpack, then to the empty water bottles—a silent demand that I pack up my shit and not leave trash on the ground, before he and Dale started back for the trail, their flashlights shifting around the path and to the surrounding woods.

I didn't argue. I didn't get mad that my brother had brought along company to the cabin when I hadn't wanted anyone there. I didn't do anything but follow Kane as he led us up the trail. I followed because that's what my brother expected.

Smug bastard.

Chapter Twelve
Kiel

The rest of the hike was quiet, except for Kane drilling Dale about Gin.

"Shit or get off the pot," Kane told his friend, earning a quick glare from the SEAL. Dale could cut one look that would leave most men nervous, but Kane knew the guy. He knew when he'd pushed too many buttons. My brother wasn't remotely done with that shit.

"The hell are you talking about?"

Kane sighed, head shaking like he couldn't believe how dense his friend was. "Funny, you don't look that dumb or blind."

Dale turned, jaw clenched, looking big and brutal as he faced my brother. "Fuck you, asshole..."

"I'm not the one who wants you to fuck them."

He meant Gin, and Dale knew it. Hell, I'd only dropped by the set a handful of times, and I still knew how bad the woman wanted him. Dale ignored the comment, flipping the bird at Kane before he walked ahead, my brother's laugh trailing behind him.

The hike served a greater purpose than Kane having the chance to fuck with his friend's head. It gave Cara the opportunity to get calm as we moved up the trail. Her expression was somber, a little sad, but she didn't complain.

For me, the silence and darkness, the monotonous movement of putting one foot in front of the other, served only to put me back on that sidewalk, cold and more terrified than I'd ever been in my life with Cara's trembling body under me.

Even in the dark, 2,850 miles from that Fifth Avenue sidewalk, I could still feel the sticky weight of blood on my fingers. The guy had sneered at me. An honest to God sneer like we were disgusting insects he took immense joy exterminating.

There was no choice.

No thought.

He'd already shot at us.

He'd already hit the driver.

He wouldn't get a chance at Cara.

One minute he was there, that asshole, full of hate and violence, likely getting off on the damage he'd done. The next, there was nothing in his eyes at all.

Just the blank nothingness and an open gaze that would never see anything at all again.

Dead. At my hands.

That had never happened to me before.

By the time we made it to the cabin, the teasing Kane had delivered to Dale was gone and the realization of what had happened to us descended like a haze that filled every available space in the small cabin.

"Kiel," Kit greeted as we walked inside, pulling me into a hug I gladly took.

"Kit," I returned, pulling back to nod at my wife. "This is Cara." She was tired, that much I made out as she tried giving Kit a weak smile. She didn't bother pretending to be polite when Gin walked into the kitchen with a case of Bud in her hands.

Like clockwork, Dale met her by the island, tugging the beer from her arm despite her small protests. "Kiel," she said, her wide smile almost was warm as Kit's. "I'm so glad y'all made it."

The women were more welcoming than Kane and Dale had been, but then, most guys I knew didn't fawn over their family and friends when they'd delivered shit right on their front steps.

"You brought her here?" Kane had said when I called him from the plane. His deep voice had been a little desperate, shocked over the cell. I'd woken him up. Knew that. Didn't much care that I had, but my brother had still managed to guilt me even half asleep. "You brought her *home*?"

"Didn't you hear me the first time?"

"Fuck, Kiel." Over the line I'd heard the rustle of fabric, then the quick slide of a zipper as Kane dressed. The door clicking behind him and his heavy feet on hardwood told me he'd wanted clear of Kit before he started screaming at me. "The fuck you bringing her here for? My God, man, what the hell am I supposed to…"

"Can you just leave some gear and clothes for us in a truck at the airport? I'll take care of getting it back down the mountain." I'd tried to keep my voice down, not liking the look of the flight attendant who kept shooting glances my way. But the plane was small, someone would catch my words no matter how low I spoke them. "We'll stay out of your hair. I don't want you messed up in this bullshit."

But Kane hadn't wanted us out of his hair. That wasn't my brother's way. It didn't surprise me. I was his kid brother. I'd always be his concern, no matter how stupid the shit I landed myself in. Still, he'd done what I'd asked and then some. Aside from the truck and gear he'd left for us, Kane had gotten the cabin ready. From the glance I'd gotten as we'd cleared the front of the cabin, Kane had made sure the wood was cut and stacked. And a quick survey of the interior and the smell permeating from the kitchen told me Kit had taken care of the rest. No need to wonder. I'd bet money there were clean linens in the closet and food in the fridge.

Kit and Gin wouldn't have it any other way. They were television DIY queens. You didn't just get fluffy towels and loaves of bread when you came to visit. You got luxury linens, towels the size of robes, dried lavender on the turned-down bed pillows, and fresh-baked bread still warm from the oven on oak cutting boards.

Kane was losing his touch. A fact that I brought to his attention when I led Cara into the cabin and stopped short, taking in the warm, cable network spread Kit had laid out for us. I sent a glance at Dale after he loaded the fridge with the beer and took the coffee mug Gin handed him.

"What the fuck is all this?" I asked Kane, motioning at the small crowd. I ignored the quick fall of Kit's smile and Gin's retreat and *definitely* how Dale shook his head at me before he retreated to the living room.

"Oh, you're welcome, asshole," Kane said, glancing for the first time at Cara. I didn't much like the look he gave her. He hadn't even acknowledged her when they met us on the trail, and now he glared at her, shooting her a look that wasn't friendly. Maybe it wasn't exactly rude, but he could have at least tried to make her feel welcome.

"Like I said. What the fuck is all this?"

"Calm down."

"Calm..." I stopped, figuring I'd take a second to settle Cara at the island and pull off my jacket before I laid into the small assembly. There was no need for explanations. Cara grabbed her lukewarm bottle of water from her jacket, and the tips of her fingers were visible underneath the bright kitchen light. Two of her fingernails had broken down to the top of her finger, and the bloodstains were more visible here. Spotting them, Kit gasped, covering her mouth and nose with her hands as she stared at the state of us.

Cara looked better than me. The loose jacket swallowed her underneath all that army-green weatherproof fabric, but she still shook, still wouldn't quite meet anyone's gaze for long. Though, I thought that might have something to do with our conversation at lunch about Kane not liking her.

"Yeah," I replied to Kit's shocked response, turning to my brother, who didn't move except for the slow flick of his eyes as he looked at my own fingers. His attention settled on my busted knuckles. "The shit we're in doesn't make company a good idea."

I glared at Dale watching me from the window along the back of the living room. "You might be able to cover your own ass, but why the hell would you let Kane talk you"—I flashed a look at Gin, then back at the SEAL—"or her into being here?"

Dale knew the score, even if he wouldn't speak it out loud. Gin was a pretty redhead with big brown eyes and a body made for trouble. Dale knew it, and he knew other men looked at her; that much I picked up the one damn time I'd tried getting Gin to let me buy her a whiskey. Dale had done so much stomping around and glaring on set that day, I decided to drop my invitation to Gin. The man was stupid for her, so why the hell would he let her tag along?

"This is a bad idea, having a house full," I told my brother, lowering my shoulders when Kit approached. She stretched her arms to offer me another hug. "Hell..." I muttered but still hugged her.

"Don't worry so much," she told me, gesturing to Kane when he tried explaining himself. At my side, Cara sat with her back straight and her arms nestled tightly around her waist. Kit followed my gaze, spotting the way Cara carried herself. How she managed to look beautiful and untouchable and utterly out of her element all at the same time. Kit winked at me, nudged Kane to the side, and stood next to Cara. "You must be so exhausted and desperate for a shower." She offered my wife a hand and smiled big when she took it.

Cara shrugged, glancing between Kit and me before she nodded. "I wouldn't hate that," she admitted.

"Good. We've got you all set up." She stepped back, nodding toward the hallway at the back of the cabin and waited as Cara looked at me, her expression unsure and wary.

"It's okay," I told her, not used to this side of her. Cara had always been a ball-busting bitch. But she'd never been attacked, not as far as I knew. She'd never been shunned by her father. This hadn't been a good week for her. That did something to me. It rattled something inside my chest that she seemed to look to me to protect her. She'd asked for that, but I'd never considered she'd meant it.

I took her hand, helping her stand. "Kit's cool, I promise. There isn't anyone in this cabin who will hurt you."

At that, Cara looked from me to Kane, and my brother caught the accusation in her expression.

"What?" he asked, face tensing as he waited for an answer. When none came, he rubbed his neck, his face brightening as though he had to say something he hadn't planned. "You expect me to promise to be okay with all this? That's not gonna happen. I remember, lady. Don't think for a second I don't. My kid brother coming home half beat to death. The way I hear it, you were the reason for that bullshit."

Kane ignored me when I rested a hand against Cara's back, letting her know I had her. Kane might be insulting, but it wouldn't go on for long, even if he kept pretending not to catch the glare I shot his way.

"Now, my kid brother gets attacked again, shot at, and carries your princess ass back here to put me and mine in danger? I won't have—"

"You know what, Kane?" Cara started, stepping closer to him, leaving my touch. "I know I fucked up. I know my family and my situation is a pain in the ass, but I was scared, stupid, and didn't know what else to do. That's why I sent for him. He protected me. He made the decision to stay because that's what you do when you make a promise." Kane opened his mouth, looking ready to argue, but Cara wouldn't let him. "You can call me a bitch and a princess and anything else you want, but get this straight. He's *my* husband, and I'm *his* wife. Whether you like it or not, I'm family. And from what your brother told me, Kainos always protect family, even if they don't deserve it."

For the first time in my life, I witnessed my brother speechless.

She wasn't exaggerating.

We stuck together.

Blood or legal ties, no matter how we became family, Kainos stuck together.

That was something Kane taught me from an early age. It was something he believed with everything in him.

Man, it had to hurt his pride to be reminded of that by someone he swore was a living hurricane set on wrecking my life.

"Well," Kit said when the quiet tension went on too long. "I freakin' like you," she told Cara. She tugged on my wife's shoulders, laughing a little at Kane's expression as Kit led Cara toward the hall. Kit stopped before she left the room, holding my brother's face between her hands and kissed him quick. "You worry too much."

Another wink thrown my way and Kit had Cara nearly out of the living room before my wife stopped, turning to look at me. "Try Johnny again. I wanna know how Arturo is." She glanced back at Kane after

I nodded at her. From the looks of it, some of her irritation had dimmed. "What I did to your brother," she started, bringing Kane's attention to her. "It was the worst thing I've ever done, and I'm not exactly from a normal American family. I've seen violence. I know heartache. But nothing I've been through ever hurt as much as what I did to Kiel. When I confess, it's the truth." And then, she left down the hallway, letting Kit lead her away from my brother's open-mouthed expression.

"Well," Gin said, following Dale as he moved out of the living room and onto the balcony. She curled her arms tightly, and Dale went to her side, placing an awkward arm over her shoulder as they stood overlooking the property, their breaths visible in the cold air when they spoke, too low for us to hear.

Kane didn't like Cara's admission, but I could see his expression shifting. The bright anger that had monopolized his face disappeared. He pushed off from the island, going to the fridge for two beers. He handed one over, then followed my gaze out to the balcony as Dale and Gin went on talking. They stood close now, closer than I'd ever seen them. I didn't make a comment or point out to Kane that his earlier suggestion for Dale to shit or get off the pot might be starting to happen. Didn't much care if it was. There were other things holding my attention.

My brother twisted off the cap of his beer and leaned against the island, eyes downcast like he needed a few long gulps to clear away the bullshit from his head. He had words for me. They were practically scattered in his eyes as he tried avoiding my attention.

The place had been well cared for since the last time I'd visited. That had been three years prior, when I'd brought some woman whose name I'd never quite remembered up here to see the first snow. The furniture hadn't changed since then; it was still lush and comfortable, with leather sofas and a tufted fabric ottoman that joined the seating area and the fireplace.

The kitchen, I figured, Kit had gotten her hands on. The cabinets were now dark and purposefully weathered, some rustic cabin-chic explosion she'd no doubt insisted on in the months since she and Kane finally got together. The cabin itself was nestled in the forest on a secluded dirt road you'd miss if you didn't it know was there. Surrounding the property were woods and a small ravine now partially frozen as the temperatures dropped and a snowstorm threatened.

The cabin was a perfect hideaway—or hideout, depending on your needs—with four decent bedrooms, three bathrooms, and a wraparound porch for great views of the land and woods surrounding it. It was ideal for keeping watch, and while I sipped my beer, waiting for my brother to speak, I realized, given our situation, that more eyes for watching was probably for the best.

I needed backup if Vinnie decided to take his threat outside the tri-state area. I had a gut feeling he did. As usual, Kane's instinct to drag Dale along was a good one. Kit and Gin, I knew, had likely been brought in for comforting Cara. Something Kane and Dale would be lousy at.

"Who's Arturo?" Kane asked, scratching the label on his beer.

"Oh, her driver. We tried getting an update on his condition with her brother on the drive up here, but the service sucks. Johnny's call dropped." I frowned, leaning against the island as I watched my brother. The man hadn't looked good when we left, but Johnny promised Cara he'd see her driver to the hospital.

"Don't worry, *bella*," he'd told his sister. "I'll do everything I can to get him good again."

Kane watched me, tilting his head when I blinked and stood away from the island. "He took a bullet just next to his collarbone. That's where all the blood came from."

My brother jerked his attention to the table, squinting at the dried blood on my knuckles. "His the only blood still sticking around?"

I didn't answer, and the quiet seemed to confirm something Kane assumed. He moved his gaze back to me, abandoning the beer as he folded his arms across his chest. "How many?"

I knew he wasn't asking about bullets left in Arturo or the number of men who had attacked us. He wanted a number that would clog up my conscience. I wouldn't give him an answer. My sins were my own. They'd stay right where they were. "You'll stay here? In case?" I asked my brother, shaking my head because he looked like he wanted to ask his question again.

But Kane didn't push. He let me keep the details to myself for now. It had been a long damn day, and I was weary.

"Dale will too," he said, eyebrows shooting up when he glanced out on the balcony to find Gin with her head on Dale's shoulder. "This...uh..." he continued, blinking as Dale stiffened his shoulders. "This is his kind of shit. It's why I brought him."

"I figured."

I polished off my beer and stretched. My limbs were aching. My muscles bunched tight from being on that damn plane. "I'm beat. You can yell at me some more in the morning." I'd made it nearly to the hallway when Kane called my name, shooting me a look I'd never seen him give me.

How much he worried, everything he did for me, all those sacrifices, somehow landed on his face. He wasn't an old man, but just then, my brother seemed ancient.

"It's good you're home. You...*and* your wife."

Chapter Thirteen
Cara

The snow had started to fall. It wasn't like the slush of wetness that collected on the sidewalks outside the museum every winter.

Washington snow was clean and fluffy and stuck to every available surface like fairy lights at Christmas. It was all around us, out on the grass, and along the forest treetops beyond the property. The snow reminded me of plumes of feathers as it fell, and I couldn't pull my attention from the other side of the window.

Behind me, the shower turned off as Kiel finished up in the bathroom, pushing heat and steam from the half-open door into the room as he moved around in there. It felt comfortable, somehow, being here in his family's cabin. It was just the two of us on the top floor. His brother and Kit took the master downstairs, and Gin got the smaller of the other bedrooms on the other side of the cabin. I was convinced that guy Dale didn't sleep at all, and if he did, it would be sitting up with his eyes wide open.

The attack was brutal and quick and made no sense to me. Johnny was sure Vinnie was responsible. "There's something that happens when a man's pride gets trampled," my brother had told me in the fleeting conversation we'd managed after landing. "I know it was him. The guy Kiel took out was Roman Atuso, Vinnie's cousin." That meant Vinnie had orchestrated the attack, likely to take out Kiel and make a place for himself in our family.

That also meant Kiel was still in danger. They'd try to come for us.

"You're not sleeping?" Kiel asked, pulling me out of my thoughts and away from the snow as he left the bathroom. He wore plaid sleep pants and nothing else. I had to turn back toward the window to avoid watching him. "I thought you were tired."

"I'm wide awake," I admitted. My blood still ran hot from everything that had happened today—the shooting, Arturo, the rush to the airport, the never-ending trek up the mountain. Maybe it was shock. Maybe I was dead inside and was too stupid to listen to my body when it wanted rest. "I tried when you were in the shower, but it's no good. Too many things on my mind."

"You're safe here," he promised, standing behind me. In the window's reflection, I caught the calm expression on Kiel's face. He meant what he said and looked like he was a little desperate for me to believe him. "No one will touch you here." He pulled my damp hair away from my neck and combed through the tangles. "Any man here would die before—"

"God, don't say that," I told him, pulling my hair from his fingers. "I don't want you or anyone else dying for me." Kiel reached for me, and I shook my head, stepping next to the bed to get space from him. He took up too much energy. "Today out on that sidewalk you covered me like you were scared I'd..."

"I was protecting you."

"You could have died!"

Before I spoke it, I hadn't realized how scared the thought made me. Kiel was my first love. He was my husband, but I'd allowed myself to keep him at a distance in my mind. If he wasn't next to me, I didn't have to worry. If he didn't speak to me, there would never be the opportunity for him to break my heart.

But now...all of that was different.

Now, there was danger and violence and the worry that he'd come back here and stay. Now there was the very real possibility that I could lose him forever, and it was entirely my fault.

We watched each other for so long I thought I could make out the flick of snow as it fell and collected outside our window. The tension felt hotter than the fireplace, and the burn in my eyes grew heavy from the assemblage of tears on my lashes.

"You could have..."

Kiel was standing in front of me in three short steps, taking hold of my shoulders like he needed me to be still and silent and listen to him for once. I didn't move.

"You wanted me to protect you..."

"I don't want you to die."

"I'm... *Shit*, Cara, you're my wife."

When it's convenient, I wanted to remind him but didn't think I could get the words out of my mouth. I didn't mean them anyway.

Kiel smoothed his hands up my shoulders, holding my face between his palms as he wiped my face dry. That kiss earlier tonight had been a tease, something to calm me. Something that had started to escalate into something I tried to pretend I didn't want. Now his eyes were so dark in the dim light of the fire. He smelled of sandalwood and fresh linen. I wanted him to kiss me and never stop. I wanted his touch, his taste, and all of him again. Not because we could die in seconds, but because we couldn't live another minute without any of it.

There was a glint in his eyes I'd seen before from him. Before the lies. Before the betrayal. Back when our lives were secret, happy, and there was a promise of the forever to come. That look gave me hope, and it kept me breathless.

"Cara," he whispered, and I willed him closer, wanting him to tilt my head toward him. Wanting the vow I'd made of us never being together again to be something I'd imagined and not real.

"Amore mio..." I took a step, sliding my hands to the back of his neck. "Kiss me like this is forever."

Kiel was a good husband. He gave. He listened, and he did what I asked. The last syllable had barely left my mouth, my nails arching slowly up his neck. Kiel released the smallest groan then took my lips because they were his.

His tongue was hot, heavy, and consumed my mouth. I let it, loving how his hold on my face shifted. How those long, perfect fingers moved from my face as he kissed me. Teasing every inch of skin they found, along my arms, down to the curve of my ass when he gripped it.

"Baby, get close," he told me, helping me lift my legs around his hips. He held me by my ass with one hand and stripped off the oversized sleepshirt Kit had given me with the other. I wore no bra underneath. Nothing at all, in fact, but that shirt. Kiel came to that realization after tossing the shirt to the floor, finding me bare, open, and so fucking wet as he walked us to the bed. "Cara... Shit..."

We went down on the bed. Kiel's wide, glorious body hovering, the small scars along his ribs shining against the firelight as he loomed over me, pulling one of my legs over his shoulder.

"You're wet, warm, and all mine," he told me, sliding to the edge of the bed. He kept my leg on that shoulder and licked my pussy, pushing on my thigh to get me wide and open.

"Warm...and sweet," Kiel said, spreading my pussy lips apart, keeping me open while he licked and sucked on my clit.

My skin felt electrified and raw, like every swipe of his tongue against me, every deep, rubbing thrust of his fingers inside me would set my skin on fire. I was sensitive everywhere, tingling, lit with something that had nothing to do with sex and touch and taste.

This time when Kiel loved me, it was because he wanted to make me feel good. Now, I wasn't a body to be used. I was the woman he loved. I felt it in every stroke of his fingers against my pussy walls, every hot lick of his tongue on my skin.

"Kiel...God," I said, gripping the sheets when he hummed against my clit, like just the taste and scent of me was the most delectable thing he'd ever had in his mouth. "Please," I tried, feeling the orgasm build. "I'm going to come...*ah*..." And he doubled his efforts, tongue working fast, fingers moving faster. I felt the tingling of my orgasm building, building, building until it sent me over the edge. I cried out, back coming off the mattress as Kiel rode the upsurge with me.

It hadn't ebbed. My entire body hummed with sensation, and Kiel did not pause or allow me a single second to regroup before he moved me back, tugging on my waist. He moved without sound. Without a single word at all. I could only watch him, running my nails over his chest and down to his stomach as he slipped off his pants and took hold of his cock in one hand.

He was beautiful, hovering over me, his thick fist rubbing up and down that perfect dick, watching me like he couldn't decide how to take me. Like the only thought that seemed clear was the undeniable need to worship me until we were both boneless.

"You ready for me, Little Goddess?" His voice was low, gravel rich. The sound of it and the sight of his flexing muscles over me were enough distraction for me not to be annoyed about the nickname.

"Always," I replied, hands still on his chest as he lowered toward me. Every second expanded. I barely managed to keep my eyes open as Kiel held himself against my pussy, teasing us both. The tip slipping between my lips, going in a little, then coming out completely.

"Fuck, I want you," he said, then stopped teasing, holding everything still except for the long, slow slip of his cock sliding into me. *"Fuck..."*

I hissed, skin lighting up again at his deep-down touch, moving my hands over his chest, up my own stomach, gripping my breasts, teasing my nipples. Kiel followed the movement, working his hips as he smoothed his hands up my ribs to squeeze both my breasts.

"More," I panted, spreading my legs farther apart. Kiel obliged, holding up my knees, speeding his hips to go deep, work harder and harder. "Yes...like that. *Just* like that..."

Kiel's grip on my legs tightened as he moved, pace steady, cock buried so deep. Then he lowered, holding one thigh apart as he came closer, lowering his mouth over mine. Stealing my breath and kiss with the mind-numbing touch of his tongue against mine. I felt him everywhere—in my pussy, pulsing hot. Against my nipples, scratching next to his chest. In my mouth as we battled for control. Kiel won, holding my head still as he continued to love me, his fingers tangled in my hair. His breath panting and damp against my face.

"Cara...oh God..." he started, hips moving faster. I knew what he wanted—that tightness, that milking surge of pressure, and when I gave it to him, Kiel threw his head back, grip tangled in the pillow next to my head. He roared, growled, and came hard deep, wet, and hot inside me.

"God...oh God," he managed. Landing on the pillow beside me, he curled one hand around my waist as he pulled me to his chest. "Fuck, baby...I love you."

I went still. Unable to keep the smile from stretching across my mouth. He didn't move when I looked up at him. Instead, Kiel's half smile only grew wider when I kissed him, pulling his face toward me.

"Mean it?" I asked. My insides hummed again when Kiel nodded, running his thumb over my face.

The next thought in my head was a reply that didn't sound rehearsed. There had been a thousand ways I'd practiced telling Kiel I loved him.

It was right there, on the tip of my tongue. Ready to admit. Ready to share. I took a breath, watching Kiel watch me, sliding my finger against the dip along his top lip. But my words froze solid like the ground outside this cabin when the power clicked off.

Those words were still there, ready to come out despite the dark quiet that surrounded us. But Kiel sat up, and the words got shoved back down as he left the bed, tugging on a pair of jeans and a thick hoodie Kane had left for him.

Then those words were forgotten completely at the shattering of both glass and silence in the cabin with the shrieking scream coming from downstairs.

Chapter Fourteen
Kiel

Dale was on point. I knew that. Logic told me maybe Gin had seen something. That had to be her screaming. Kane had mumbled something to me before I came upstairs about Dale taking first watch, with Gin keeping him company. A half thought-of joke ran through my mind about them together, alone, but everything save for that scream got squashed. I found the Glock in the bedside table where I'd left it and moved away from the bed.

"Stay here," I told Cara, frowning when she only stared back at me. She was defiant. Stubborn. She didn't like anyone telling her what to do, but there was real fear on her face just then. She was terrified. "Baby, please," I said, kissing her forehead. "If you were ever gonna listen to me, now is the time. Don't fucking leave this room, okay?"

The nod was quick. Something I didn't buy in the least, but there was no time to demand a pinkie promise from my wife. The thundering of feet was loud, and I needed to find out what the hell was waiting for me downstairs.

"Shit gets sideways, you fucking hide, Cara. I mean it."

"Kiel..." she started, the sharp, desperate tone of her voice stopping me. Cara held her breath, blanket pulled up across her chest as I glanced back at her. "I...I love you too."

Half a second was all I could spare, but her expression and the tone of her voice had me stuck where I stood. I'd waited a long time to hear that from her again. It was here now, but there was no time to enjoy it. Instead, I nodded, forcing myself to step toward the door before I answered her. The need to touch her nearly overwhelmed me, but I managed to keep myself in check. "I know you do, baby." And then I shot out of the door.

The hall was pitch-black and silent. The rustling feet I'd heard seconds before had quieted, and now there was nothing moving in the cabin.

Not even the gust of storm wind from an hour before was rushing anymore. It was as if the world had gone silent. As if everything—the heavy tree limbs, the manic wind, the running water from the creek outside, the crowing wildlife, the mountain itself had all decided to hold its breath and wait for whatever inevitability was about to happen.

It didn't fill me with comfort. Fear leveled up inside me, like bricks against a flimsy gate. All the anxiety, worry, and dread inside me crashed together.

But then the memory shot through me again—Cara underneath me, her entire body shaking like a Chihuahua stuck in a rainstorm as bullets rang out over our heads. Then the image of her open to me minutes before, letting me love her and take her and giving me everything she had, eradicated that worry.

It squashed the dread.

In its place came anger and the burning itch to lay flat the playing field.

I would not let Vinnie take what was mine.

What would always be mine.

I wouldn't let anyone keep her from me ever again.

There were no creaks or noises on the steps as I took them. No movement down in the living room as I descended the stairs, but I caught a shadow moving across from me, something looming and stiff. I gripped the gun tighter, flipping off the safety as I aimed it toward the shadow.

The shadow danced against the full, bright moon, and I squeezed the handle of my Glock, aiming with my hand held out, ready to shoot as I tilted toward the corner of the wall. But I found only Gin huddled against the back of the sofa, knees to her chest as she cupped her face in her hands.

"Dale..." I heard. The whisper was soft, pained, but echoed across the kitchen when Gin spoke it. The woman was fierce on a good day. She was a licensed contractor used to the bullshit women working in a male-dominated field usually got. But Gin held her own most of the time, from what Kane had mentioned, showing the boys how it was done. She was not a woman who scared easily. But that tone had me second-guessing whose voice I heard.

"Please, not Dale...no."

She jolted but stayed silent when I darted to her, holding my fingers over her mouth before she could scream.

"Where?" I whispered, shoulder to shoulder with her when something rustled outside. The sound was muffled by the glass doors, but I could still make out the thud of moving bodies.

"Dale heard something." Gin's voice was low, raspy, and she leaned toward my ear as she spoke. "He went out to the balcony and saw...something or someone. He...he screamed at me to get inside and lock the doors." She wiped her wet face as though she was irritated she cried but continued. "I'd just gotten the lock bolted when I saw two assholes tackle him to the ground. I was going to run up and get Kane, but then..." She nodded, and when I followed her gaze, my stomach sank.

I immediately darted toward the kitchen, only to be stopped when my brother's look held me back.

Kane was slumped against the kitchen island and had one of Vinnie's assholes in a headlock. The man wasn't giving up and fought hard, making weak attempts to twist away from my brother, angling his elbow up to jab at Kane's ribs, but that move was deflected quick. Kane was large and flexible with the asshole around the neck. His long legs locked around the guy's thighs, squeezing him tight.

Another step and Kane glared at me, shaking his head. "Mine," he wheezed, and I backed off, getting distracted by the tussle when another thump of noise sounded on the other side of the glass doors.

"Dale!" Gin screamed when the man in question was thrown against the glass, ducking as one beefy asshole swung at him. He could handle himself but didn't need to.

"Go!" I yelled at Gin, jerking my head toward the stairs. "Stay with Cara and..."

"Kane?" I heard over my shoulder. It never fucking failed. Always something. Always a threat when there shouldn't have been one. Kane should have left me to this. But then I'd have been left on my own with only my scared wife to back me up. I squashed the regret and darted toward a terrified-looking Kit as she came into the kitchen. "What..."

"Kiel!" my brother called.

I took it for the warning it was, pulling both Gin and Kit out of the room and hustling them up the stairs. "Stay here. Don't come down for anything." I knocked against the door, and Cara opened it wide, ushering in Kit and Gin. "Do *not* leave this room."

"But Kane..." Kit tried, and my headshake kept her quiet.

"You feel threatened, you run. Back stairs on the other side of the landing," I reminded Kit.

The cabin had been renovated when we bought it, but Kane hadn't wanted to take out the stairs in case of some dumb-luck emergency. Didn't figure he was thinking of a mafia attack.

"There's a shed about a hundred feet on the other side of the creek," I told them. "Get in there and stay put until we come for you, but do not leave unless you have to."

"Kane..." Kit tried again, glancing at Gin when the redhead grabbed her arm. "And Dale..."

"I'll figure out what's going on, don't worry." I spared one last look at my wife, then at the other women before I started down the stairs. "Lock the door," I called behind me and didn't exhale until I heard the door shut and the lock engage.

The noise in the kitchen had gone quiet by the time I jogged back down the stairs, holding my breath over how my brother was faring. I spotted him, pushing the unconscious body of the bastard he'd been fighting on his stomach. Kane snapped up straight, shoulders tight when I hit the last step. He immediately shot a look toward the door upstairs before he glanced at me. I wondered for a second how much blame he laid at my feet. I'd asked for help. I'd brought trouble back home with me, but Kane had welcomed it. He'd brought his people around it willingly. But the guilt felt like a weight hanging around my neck.

"Kane..."

"They'll be fine," my brother said, slapping my shoulder before another thump of noise sounded. Dale threw one of Vinnie's assholes against the glass. "These motherfuckers though..."

"Come on," I told him, running toward the glass doors.

A lot happened at once. So much that I only caught half of what went down. The noise, the lick of frigid air that hit my arms and the back of my neck, the tumble of bodies all got jumbled inside my head the second I led my brother out of the cabin and onto the balcony.

Dale clocked the biggest of the two assholes who staggered around him, and fleetingly, I thought I'd underestimated what a badass the man was. But then Kane met another guy shooting right for us. I spotted Vinnie climbing the steps, and everything around me, the people who were fighting because of me, all paused.

"Motherfucker," I growled as Vinnie landed on the deck. I forgot the Glock in my hand long enough that when Vinnie came at me, his own gun aimed, I managed to deflect him, slamming my piece against his arm.

"*Bastardo!*" he shouted as his gun flew across the deck. I caught his meaning and ignored it, ducking when he took a swing at me.

The asshole was lithe. Quicker than me and when he doubled back, taking another swing, he moved fast enough that he caught my chin. My head snapped back, and I wobbled against the glass door. It flew open, and Vinnie charged at my middle, catching me off guard, sacking me like a linebacker. We crashed inside, landing on the small side table next to the sofa.

Outside, I heard Dale screaming at whoever he fought and Kane trading licks with the two bodyguards that seemed to still be standing. But Vinnie scrambled over me, and I refocused, pushing him off me as we both shoved to our feet.

"You take what's mine, *sì*? Take what's owed me?" he said, his accent thick, barely audible as he panted.

"Nothing here is yours, asshole." He came at me, and I smiled, jerking to the side to land a fist right at the bastard's rib.

He whined, crying out in pain just as Dale and Kane staggered through the door, both gathering up the guns that had fallen in the tussles on the balcony. It only took a second of distraction before hell came rushing forward.

Kane leaned against the wall, breaths heavy, and Dale stood straight, alert, right next to me, stuffing one of the guns in his hands into his waistband as Vinnie bent over, clutching himself.

"You good?" I asked them, getting nods in return, and then Vinnie straightened, darting forward to grab the gun in Dale's hand.

The asshole laughed, stepping back as he aimed the gun between me and Dale.

"Calm down," I told Vinnie, but the man looked wired, a little desperate. He didn't seem able to do anything but curse under his breath, words I knew were insults but couldn't identify. "Vinnie..."

"Fuck you, Kaino," he spat, squeezing the trigger.

Chapter Fifteen
Cara

There were promises, and there were *promises*. It was hard keeping them, even to a man like Kiel. The only sound in the room was the whispers between Gin and Kit and the grumbles both women made as the world sounded like it was unraveling below us. My father's business was violent. Sometimes that violence carried over, made noises I couldn't help but overhear in late-night hours when he thought I was sleeping. I was used to violent noises. But none of them had ever scared me like the ones I heard just then.

None of them had ever threatened my husband.

"I can't just sit here wondering and waiting," Gin said. The woman's face was pale, her expression tight. She kept popping her knuckles, a nervous habit that got under my skin. "This is total bullshit," she said, getting up from the bed to dart toward the door for the third time. "I can't..."

"You wanna get shot?" I asked her, dropping any pretense of being friendly to either of these women. They might be family or close to it to Kiel, but that didn't mean I had to play nice just because they were scared. "Or worse, you wanna distract your man so that he glances at you and drops his guard? Easy way for those bastards to get the upper hand."

"No. Of course not," Kit said, her voice soothing, matching the way she squeezed her friend's hand. Gin tossed me a glance then shook her head.

"This is bad, I know." The women frowned at me, and I hurried to correct myself. I might not have to play nice, but there was no need to get them all worked up and itching to throw open the door and dart right into the middle of whatever was happening downstairs. "I know rough men. I can tell when one can handle himself. Those three will have no problems..."

The telltale rip of a bullet shot through the quiet below and cut off whatever bullshit I was planning to say. Damn the danger. Damn the promises I'd made to Kiel. We three spared one glance at each other then clamored for the door, struggling to open it.

The noise had started up again, and from our vantage point, we spotted the small crowd downstairs. Vinnie gestured with a gun like a maniac, pointing it at Kane as he moved to Dale, who was bent over on the floor, clutching his side.

"Back up, *stronzo*," Vinnie told Kane.

"He's down. I have to—"

"You have to do nothing. Move away..."

Behind me, Kit and Gin struggled, trying to maneuver away from me to get to their men, but I managed to keep them back. "Hold on," I whispered, my heart thundering against my ribs. "He's got a gun."

"Dale..." Gin started, leaning against me. I felt her hot tears on my back as she gripped my arm. "Oh God, please..."

"Move. Now," Vinnie tried again, twisting his gun to angle it at Kiel. I stopped breathing as he sidestepped, going toward his brother and their downed friend.

"Dale?" Kane called, focus still on a shaking Vinnie.

"I'm...good," the man wheezed, but his breath was labored. The pain he felt was evident in the low breath he released. When Dale leaned back, rolling to his back and slumping on the floor, blood spilling from his side, I couldn't keep Gin back. She gasped, bringing the attention of the men right up at her.

Vinnie's mouth hardened, and a smug, pleased smile broke across his face. *"Bella,"* he said, laughing as he pointed the gun right at Kiel's chest. "Come here." When I didn't move, the man narrowed his eyes, moving his top lip in a curl. He stepped forward, pushing the gun right over Kiel's heart. "Now, *bella*."

"Cara," Kiel warned, face set hard.

I came down the stairs, holding a hand up when Gin tried scrambling around me to get at Dale.

"Careful," Vinnie told her, nodding for both her and Kit to stay back. "I will take Cara, sì, back to her papa."

"Like hell," Kiel said, flinching when Vinnie's gun moved, twisting into his chest. He stepped forward, sticking his chest out. "Do it," he taunted, face screwed up in a snarl. "Because it's only over my dead fucking body that you'll take my wife back to New York."

"Kiel, no," I cried. My heart was beating so fast now that I got light-headed.

"Understood," Vinnie said.

My focus was on Vinnie's finger curled around the trigger and the slow-motion movement of him squeezing it. The scream left my mouth. I curled my hands over my ears just as Kiel slapped Vinnie's hand away and the gun fired just over my husband's head.

Everything happened in beats, like what I saw came out in slow, jarring segments, a paradox of stillness and rapid-fire movements. Vinnie stumbled back as Kiel grabbed his collar, pulling him near the door and the balcony beyond it. Gin escaped the stairs and ran straight for Dale, wailing out an awful noise that was more growl than scream. Kane launched himself at Kit, arms outstretched as he went for her just as the half-conscious asshole near the island came to, observed the chaos around him, then scrambled to his feet, charging right at Kane. He slammed into the big man, knocking him to the floor, and Kane released a loud rush of air from his chest as he fell on top of the coffee table, splintering the wood.

I didn't know Gin and Kit well. They were practically strangers I'd been forced upon like a stray puppy in an at-capacity kennel because of our circumstance. But each of us was scared. Each of us terrified of what happened around us to the men we loved.

Dale was down and bloody, and Gin didn't seem able to do more than shake and make weak attempts at comforting him. Kit was screaming at her downed man as some asshole pummeled him, and I could only stare, breath held, as Kiel traded punches with Vinnie out on the balcony.

It took the briefest glance between the three of us before we moved, but there was a clarity in that moment that made me almost believe in some cosmic surge that moved between women. Our men were threatened. We were scared, but none of us seemed able to cower under a table or behind closed doors waiting for a rescue.

Kit moved in time with me, and Gin followed. The bastard beating on Kane stood up straight, ready to deliver another punch, then stopped short as we came at him. There were cuts and scrapes all over his face, and his left eye was swollen shut. But shock was easy to make out, even on a bruised and bloody face like his.

Kane groaned on the floor, and we toppled the bastard, Kit getting the most traction as she jumped on his back and started beating her fists against his head. I followed, clawing at the bastard's neck just as Gin clamored around his front, driving her knee up into his crotch.

"Fuck!" he cried, trying and failing to cover his head as we beat, slapped, and clawed over every free inch of skin we found. It went on forever, the sounds of his loud cries getting louder and more desperate the more we beat on him. He called out names we didn't know, men I guessed had come along for the attack, but only Vinnie was still moving, and his attention was taken up by Kiel. "Get off...oh! God!" the bastard cried as he went to his knees, giving up fighting us off and settling for burying his face against the area rug covered in the splinters of the coffee table.

"You got him," Kane wheezed, pushing off the floor, sounding proud as he pulled Kit away from the downed asshole. "Baby, come on." She climbed off him, and Gin retreated to Dale as I got to my feet, watching Kiel and Vinnie on the balcony. Kane stood behind me, moving his large hand to my shoulder as if to stop me from disrupting the fight. "He'll be okay. Trust me."

I didn't have Kane's confidence in Kiel, but then, I'd only heard from Johnny how the Kiel I'd betrayed five years ago hadn't been much of a fighter when they'd cornered him.

This Kiel, however, was scary.

"That all you got, motherfucker?" he yelled at Vinnie when the man landed one solid punch against Kiel's chin. They both staggered, but Vinnie was the one struggling to stand upright. He was bulky and strong, but Kiel was stronger.

"Fuck you!" Vinnie screamed, wiping blood from his nose as he charged at Kiel, managing to knock him to his knees and against the firepit near the center of the balcony.

"Wrong answer," Kiel said, rolling to his side to grab the metal fire poker leaning against the railing. He had it in his grip, turning it before Vinnie noticed it, and Kiel brought the metal poker down against Vinnie's knee, then right at his ankle. Two loud, crunching strikes against his body and the bastard went down, grabbing his fresh injury as Kiel got to his feet.

Kane let me go as I rushed toward the door, watching Kiel stand over the man, that poker still gripped in his massive fist. He watched Vinnie wailing and panting on the floor, and something moved across his face—rage and anger and likely a lot of hatred.

It reminded me of how my father's men looked after coming back from *appointments* I knew were code for family "business." Violence slipped into the shadows of their eyes, and it hung around them like fog.

That had started to creep into Kiel's features, and the sight of it scared me. He wasn't one of my father's brutal guards. He was talented. Kiel was intelligent, and he was *mine*. He was nothing like the men I'd been around my entire life. It was why I loved him.

That fist gripped the poker tighter, and Kiel moved his hand, like he was considering smashing Vinnie's face in just to make sure the asshole never came after us again. But when I stepped onto the balcony and caught Kiel's attention, he glanced at me. He blinked, lashes fanning quick, as though just that rapid action was enough to pull that haze of violence from his head.

"Amore mio," I said, my voice sounding thick with the tears I forced down my throat. He nodded, glancing once at Vinnie, who was barely conscious, before Kiel threw the poker over the railing and darted toward me, engulfing me in his large arms.

"Baby," he whispered with a relieved breath before he held my face between his hands. Kiel ignored Kane as he came out onto the balcony to hustle Vinnie inside. I didn't care what the big man did to him. The only thing that held my attention was the warmth of Kiel's hands against my cheeks and the taste of his mouth when he kissed me. "I told you to stay in that room." I could only shrug, having no excuses that would keep him from complaining. "You're the most stubborn woman I've ever known."

"But you still love me?" I asked, inhaling the scent of his skin as he held me.

"I damn well do, goddess." Then Kiel kissed me long and slow like our world hadn't just been toppled. Like there was no one else on the planet but me and my beautiful husband.

Chapter Sixteen
Kiel

Picking at the dried blood on my hands, I closed my eyes and leaned against the wall next to Kane. The girls were clustered together across the room, giving Gin as much comfort as possible as we waited for word on Dale. We were all banged up and covered in blood, some of which wasn't our own. Dale had gotten the worst of it, though. The gunshot required a surgery that we'd finally got word he made it through.

Kane has barely spoken ten words to anyone since we'd settled into the waiting room. The guilt felt like a noose around my neck, choking me the deeper my brother's frown got. We were here because of me. Dale would still be standing, not lying in a hospital bed, if it weren't for my getting involved with Cara again. I rubbed my face, massaging at my temples to get the headache to ease, but it was no use. That guilt filled me and made breathing difficult. We should've stayed in New York and let Cara's family handle things, instead of bringing the trouble to my brother's doorstep.

"This is some bullshit." Kane pushed himself off the wall. My eyes followed his path, spinning on his heels before he stalked back toward me. Kit raised her head, giving Kane a sad smile before she tightened her hold on Gin. "It shouldn't be taking so long," Kane grumbled, unaffected by Kit's momentary gaze. I knew my brother. It didn't matter what assurances the doctors gave us. Kane wouldn't relax until he saw Dale for himself.

"I'm sorry." The words came out in a rush, making my brother shoot a look at me. I couldn't decipher the expression he wore. The apology was sincere and the only words I seemed able to manage. Couldn't he tell? Couldn't any of them? "If I could switch places, I'd take it. This is on me."

I shouldn't have agitated Vinnie, but I couldn't stop myself. Cara was mine. No one threatened anyone I loved. Especially not my wife.

"Don't be a dick." Kane shook his head as he kept pacing.

"I'm not being a dick, asshole."

"The last thing I need is you lying in that bed."

I blew out a breath, knowing he was right, but that didn't make the sting any easier. "We should've stayed in New York."

At least in New York, we had Cara's family and all their goons to protect us. Vinnie and his men wouldn't have gotten within fifty feet of us, but we would've been prisoners at her father's compound. If we'd stayed, I probably would've ended up dead, a casualty of the war I'd never wanted or asked for.

Kane stalked toward me and grabbed me by the shoulder. "Stop your nonsense. You're right where you should be." He shook me, almost making me bang my head on the wall behind me. "Do you fucking hear me?" His eyes burned, simmering rage and fear clouding their depths. The emotion wasn't something I often saw in him, but it was unmistakable when I did.

"I hear ya," I muttered, but I wasn't convinced. We wouldn't be at the hospital right now if I'd kept my ass put instead of dragging Cara all the way across the country with me.

"Dale knew what he was getting into. The man is tougher than anyone I know. He's going to be fine."

I wondered if he said the words for me or to comfort himself, but I didn't bother asking. "You look like shit," I said because I didn't have anything else worth saying. We all looked like we'd been to hell and back.

"Feel like it too." He almost cracked a smile. "Listen, I'll take care of the cops. I know they're probably on their way."

"Fuck. We better get our story straight." I hadn't even thought about the police or the media who would be on this story once they heard my brother was involved.

"It was a horrible hunting accident gone wrong," he told me. "You hear me?" He waited a minute, long enough for me to nod before he continued. "I don't want anyone going up there while we wait for Johnny."

"Understood. Who shot Dale?" I asked because there was no way I wanted to be the one to fuck up the lie.

"Can't tell. We both were by each other's side and shot in the same direction, not knowing he was across the field."

"You think that shit will fly?"

"It'll work. Shit like that happens every day."

"But..." I said, glancing down at our torn clothes covered in blood from the fight with Vinnie's men.

"Dale's blood. Tears are from when we carried him through the thick forest."

I shrugged, figuring his explanation worked, and between the story and his celebrity, the cops wouldn't dig too deep. We didn't have to worry about the Seattle police knowing Cara or the trouble her family brought with the name, so at least that point wasn't a dead giveaway.

The nurse walked into the room, a metal binder clutched in her hands as she scanned the name, calling "the Reynolds family," with her eyes still on the chart. She moved her gaze around the waiting room, only half filled with impatient families then nodded when Gin shot up, darting toward her.

Kane followed behind Gin, raising his hand. "We're here."

She nodded and gave him and Kit a quick smile when they joined Gin. The woman ignored everyone but my brother and his woman, likely recognizing them like most everybody around here did. "He's settled in his room now and finally coming out of the anesthesia. You can go up. He's in room 417."

She barely got the number out before Gin was in the hallway, Kane, with Kit at his side, hot on her heels. I grabbed Cara, placing my hand at the small of her back, and walked behind them, keeping silent because I hadn't processed everything yet. The hospital wasn't the place to discuss what happened and how we were going to deal with the situation still at the house.

Kane froze as we stepped off the elevator, and my eyes followed his gaze. *Fuck.*

"Let me handle everything," Kane told us, straightening his shoulders and stepping in front of Gin. "Not a word from any of you."

"I'll help," I called out, but he turned around and growled. "Let's go, ladies," I said, sweeping my arms out and ushering them away from the officers and inside.

A woman stood over Dale's bed dressed in scrubs, holding his hand like they were having a moment.

"What the fuck?" Gin whispered as her body tensed, throwing my hand off her shoulder.

The woman turned and glared at Gin. Clearly, they knew each other, but I had no idea from where. "Gin," the woman said, lifting her chin as her eyes raked down the redhead's body.

Gin stepped forward, her hands at her sides but balled tight like she was about to go off and clock the nurse right in the face. "You shouldn't be here, Trudy."

Trudy crossed her arms, tilting her head with a sneer, acting as though she didn't give two shits if Gin was going to hit her. "He's my husband. I have every right to be here."

I rocked back on my heels, glancing down at Cara, who looked just as shocked as me. I'd heard of Trudy. Dale never had a thing good to say about her, and I understood why. She'd been a lousy wife, and now was a piece of trash Dale couldn't get loose from. Dale hated her, but he never said much else except for the one time we got him so drunk he spilled the entire dirty story.

"Your *ex*-husband," Gin corrected her as she moved to the foot of Dale's bed.

If the room hadn't been so crowded with unwanted hospital employees, I'd have thought the expression on Dale's face was hilarious when he began to stir. There was a lazy, goofy grin pulling up his mouth, and by the way he laughed and waggled his eyebrows at us, it was clear the man was still high as a kite from the anesthesia.

His gaze moved between the two women, but he didn't speak or try to defuse the situation. There was nothing to do but watch the drama unfold. This would be bad. I could feel it in my gut. Very fucking bad. At times like this, with two women about to throw down, my brother needed to be here.

"Ladies," I said and stepped forward, ready to give it a shot. "Maybe we should..."

"Who the fuck are you?" Dale's ex-wife asked, turning her icy glare toward me.

"Get the fuck out," Gin told Trudy before I had a chance to answer.

"Baby," Trudy turned toward Dale, grabbing his hand again, "do you want me to go?" she asked, her voice so sugary sweet it gave me a toothache. This bitch was good and knew exactly what she was doing.

Dale blinked slowly and out of sync, pressing his head back into the pillow that looked entirely too small behind his head. "Nah, baby." He brought Trudy's hand to his lips and kissed her knuckles. "You're my wife."

Oh fuck.

That one word seemed to do nearly as much damage to Gin as the bullets Vinnie had shot into Dale's gut. Eyebrows up in surprise, I couldn't move my head, too shocked and too worried what would happen next. A few seconds later, I glanced around to the shocked faces surrounding me as the air seemed to rush from the room. Dale was going to hate himself once the meds wore off and he realized how badly he fucked up.

"See." Trudy grinned, reminding me of a girlie, petty Cheshire cat as she kept her hand in his, letting him kiss her repeatedly. "I have every right to be here. Don't I, baby?" She used a voice that reminded me of the forced sweetness dripping from my little cousin's preschool teachers back in the day. The sound made bile rise in the back of my throat.

Gin's expression could only be described as seething. Her pale skin brightened to a pink, and her neck and chest flushed. If that bitch kept fake smiling at the redhead the way she was, someone was gonna get hurt. I'd put money on Gin winning any day of the week.

Needing to do something before security was called, I moved toward Trudy, grabbing her by the arm, forceful but not cruel. "You need to leave." She struggled against me as I moved her away from Dale.

"You going to make me?" She laughed. "I work here. You're the one that's going to leave. Not me."

"I can't," Gin said, covering her mouth as her eyes filled with tears.

"Gin." Kit reached for her, but Gin batted her hands away and rushed out the door. "Fuck me," Kit hissed and rubbed her hand down her face, knowing the shitstorm this was going to cause later, just like I did. Kit exhaled as she moved toward Trudy. "You're a bitch, Trudy. Nothing but a trashy whore. You'd better get the hell out of here before I kick your ass."

"Kiel, why the hell've you got your hands on my woman?" Dale asked, and everyone in the room turned toward him.

The guy, as big as he was, looked small somehow on that bed, his beard a scruffy mess. Those eyes seemed brighter somehow, the blue shining against the fluorescent light above. And when he narrowed his eyes, top lip curled as he looked at my hand on Trudy's arm, despite his stupid grin, I shook my head. No way he knew what he was saying. Not as high as he was. The man hated this woman, but his question still had the faces around the room looking shocked, disbelieving, except for Trudy, who seemed to relish the compliment, soaking it up like the bitch Dale had promised she was.

I dropped my hand from her arm, defusing the situation so he wouldn't try to climb out of the bed. An agitated Dale wasn't a good thing, especially right after surgery. He had enough meds in him he probably felt like Superman. "Dude, shut the fuck up."

He made a face at me, mocking the way I spoke as he latched on to Trudy's hand again, yanking her toward him. "I've missed you," he said, staring at her with puppy-dog eyes.

I glanced up at the ceiling and scrubbed my hand down my face, cursing under my breath at the stupidity of the entire situation. What the hell was taking my brother so long? He'd know what to do. He'd wrangle everybody in.

"Why did Gin run out of here?" Kane asked, entering the room behind me on heavy footsteps. "Oh hell no. Not happening," he said, moving quickly.

Kane walked right past me and stood toe-to-toe with Trudy, shooting a glare at her that had to make the woman nervous. "Get the fuck out." He took a step, and the woman walked backward, looking at Dale on the bed, then around to the rest of us as though we might help. "It's time for you to find some other dick to jump on. Your gravy train ended a long time ago."

"Kane." Dale smiled again, his mouth lopsided. "Look who showed up. It's my wife." He seemed just as shocked as the rest of us to see her, but happy...and high.

"Shut up, Dale," Kane growled.

Kit grabbed Trudy by the arm and moved her hand away from Dale. "Honey, there's no room for you in his life. You either leave, or I'm going to make you."

This was a side I didn't often see from Kit, but I liked every damn second of it. She was fiery and a perfect match for my brother. She kind of reminded me of Cara. Neither my brother nor I liked our women weak, and we paid for that shit too.

Trudy tipped her head back, almost cackling. "He wants me here. I can't leave him when he needs me."

Cara slid against my side, curling into my ribs and placing her hand on my stomach. "My money's on Kit," she whispered, staring up at me as I looked down, kissing her forehead.

Kit twisted Trudy's arm, ignoring how the woman whined as she shoved her toward the door. "I'm taking out the trash," she said, smiling as Trudy tried to get away, but Kit's grip was just too tough.

"Holy shit," I whispered and reminded myself never to mess with Kit. She hauled that girl outside like she was a tiny kid throwing a temper tantrum.

"She's small but mighty," Kane said as I stood there with Cara in my arms and my mouth hanging open. "How bad is the damage?"

"Doctor hasn't come in yet."

Kane pressed his fingers against his eyes and shook his head. "No, dumbass. Dale. What'd he say?"

"You don't want to know, brother."

"Bad," Cara said. "*Really* bad."

"Fuck." Kane rubbed the back of his neck, pacing on the side of Dale's bed. "You dumb fuck. I can't believe after all this time you..."

Dale blinked a few times before he rubbed his eyes with the sides of his fists. "What'd I do?"

"Trudy." Kane motioned toward the door. "I never thought you'd go down that road again."

"Kane, he's drugged, man. Give him a break," I said. I'd been there, and you couldn't control the shit that came out of your mouth after surgery. It was worse than being drunk.

"Tomorrow he's going to wish that bullet killed him." I nodded in agreement before Kane turned back toward Dale. "Thank God you're okay. I can't imagine if..." He didn't finish the statement. He didn't have to. We were all thinking the same thing.

"Where's Gin?" Dale asked, finally sobering up, but a little too late to avoid causing massive damage. "Gotta see my Gingerbread."

"Oh boy." Cara's hand slipped under my shirt, her fingernails tracing the dip in my spine. "This is going to get interesting."

Kane looked at Dale with a straight face. "You better get well quick, 'cause you're going to be on your knees groveling to fix this shit."

"Fix what?" Dale asked, jerking his head back and wincing in pain.

"You'll see."

Chapter Seventeen
Cara

The trek back up the mountain wasn't the easy trip it had been the first night Kiel brought me here. A light blanket of snow had collected and stuck to the ground the night before, and ice had formed along the creek. But there was nothing to be done. We'd been found out.

The flight attendant, it turned out, had been bought off the second I canceled plans with Vinnie the first time. He'd been wary, I supposed, and had set about trying to bribe everyone affiliated with my family. The night janitor at the museum, my father's newest driver, the new flight attendant, all had been paid to keep the asshole up to date with where I went and who came with me.

The woman had been confronted, Johnny informed me when he called the next morning after the attack. "She paid off the parking attendant who'd overheard Kiel mention the cabin. Didn't take much for Vinnie to find out the location."

Also didn't take much for the news to break that cable TV's darling DIYers had been caught up in a shooting accident, as Kit and Kane's handlers were spinning it. That meant media. That meant invasive questions and virtually no privacy at the hospital, any Seattle hotels, or at Kane's, Kit's, Gin's, or Dale's places.

"Go back to the cabin," my brother had suggested, sounding confident that no one would put up much of a fight. "I'll handle the security."

If Johnny had ideas about who should watch over us, he didn't share them or even encourage much relief as all of us, excluding Dale who still had a few more days in the hospital, made the slow hike toward the cabin.

"Dale will never be able to swing this without the ATV," Kane remarked, wincing a little as he moved up the trail in front of us.

"Or, we'll luck out, and Dale will stay in Seattle," Gin supplied, her anger still fierce and prickling through the frown she wore and the bite in her tone. "Or he can rot in freakin' hell where he belongs." She brushed off the pat Kit gave her and moved ahead of us.

"Shit, does she have a temper or what?" Kiel said, sounding half amazed.

"You got no idea," Kit answered.

When the cabin came into view and we spotted the small congregation of men flanked out around the property, we all stopped. Even Gin backed away despite her anger and waited for Kane and Kiel to take the lead. There were at least a dozen men in dark jeans and thick black coats circling the edge of the property line and along the back of the cabin. They wore shades, all of them, and didn't react when the Kaino men started up the stairs, nodding us along.

"The hell?" Kane started, then went quiet as we entered the cabin. He whistled, head shaking as we moved inside. "Unbelievable."

We'd left the place in a mess. Blood had left stains on the walnut floors and splinters of wood and glass were scattered around the room and embedded into the wool area rug. There were balcony chairs askew and upturned stools left on their sides or broken altogether. We'd had no time to tidy a thing.

Now, though, nothing was out of place. There were no stains, no broken glass, or splintered wood. The rug was spotless, freshly shampooed from the looks of it, and the broken island stools and balcony chairs had all been replaced or repaired.

As we came farther inside, all fascinated by the cleanliness of the place, I spotted the open glass door, exhaling when I noticed my brother Johnny leaning against the railing, flicking ashes from his cigar over the side.

He was impossibly annoying and a huge pain in the ass, but he was still my big brother. I loved him, the big jackass, and I didn't stop myself when my feet moved, jogging toward him. He turned, arms spread wide to pull me into his embrace.

"Ah, *rella*," he soothed, giving me a tight squeeze and a kiss on the head. Immediately, I flushed, realizing just how relieved my brother was. When we were kids, he couldn't pronounce his S's very well so "sorella," Italian for sister, came out as "rella." He only called me that when he wanted me to know how much he loved me. But Johnny was a macho asshole too. Bossy beyond belief and the hug was paused as he pushed me back, holding my arms outstretched as he fussed over me, examining, clicking his tongue, head shaking. "You could have been killed! *Cazzo*, Cara."

"Shut up," I told him, laying my head against his chest again. There had been so much blood, and more than once during the past few days, I'd wondered if there would ever be a chance for me to see my brother again. I wondered if the last words my papa ever spoke to me would be the demand that I leave his house. "Just hug me a little, you *stronzo*."

"Hell," Johnny breathed. He curved his arms around me as he whispered low, private things I'd never heard him speak to anyone.

Behind us, Kiel cleared his throat, bringing my attention back to him. I stepped away from my brother and went to Kiel's side as Kane joined us on the balcony. "You put that shit out, and we can have a conversation inside, Carelli," Kane offered, and my brother stiffened, barely moving his head to acknowledge my brother-in-law.

We moved out of the cold and into the clean living room as Johnny followed, shutting the glass door behind him. He kept watch on the balcony, his gaze shooting out to the snow-capped trees and the creek in the distance.

"It's nice," Johnny started, finally turning to face Kiel and his brother. At the kitchen island, Gin had already cracked open a bottle of red, and Kit was helping her with the glasses. My brother nodded behind him, standing in the center of the room, his hands deep in his pockets. "Quiet? No one bothering you?" Kane nodded but didn't speak otherwise, something Johnny seemed fine with.

"Know what's bothering *me*?" Gin asked behind a sip of wine. She stared at Johnny. I caught a small twitch in his cheek as he looked at her.

"What's that, *bella*?"

The redhead paused, as though she wasn't used to anyone using endearments on her, but then gripped her wineglass and frowned at my brother. "This," she said, waving her glass around the room. "I want to be in my own bed, back in the city. I want to get away from the forest and fucking..." She paused, searching for a word I guessed she hoped wouldn't be insulting before she continued. "*People*...certain kinds of gun-firing people."

That comment amused my brother. He didn't bother holding back his smile. "Gun-firing people?" he asked, moving a few feet to get nearer to Gin. "You mean people...like me?"

"People..."

"With a certain kind of business," Kit tried, dropping her smile when Kane glared at her. "What?"

"Dirty business," Kane said, interrupting. "Your business, Carelli. The kind that landed on my doorstep."

"*Si,*" he said, motioning like Kane's concern didn't matter. "First thing's first." He tilted his head, watching Gin as she went on downing the red. "I'm sorry about insisting everyone stay here. It was necessary." Johnny stood across the island from Gin, holding her stare with one of his flirty smirks.

What an ass my brother was. He was handsome, a little too handsome, and he knew it. He'd throw a smile, give away a wink, and women seemed to crumble around him. Ridiculous. Embarrassing, and at the moment, useful. Gin hadn't released any of her anger since Dale's slipup at the hospital. We could use a distraction from her sullen mood.

"The cabin is up high enough that we'll see anyone coming who might try pulling out a lens to get an exclusive." He grabbed the bottle, offering to refill Gin's glass, and she let him, unable to do anything but angle her chin in thanks. Johnny didn't take his gaze from her face as he poured the wine. "The property," he continued, still watching her, "is large enough that my men can cover each opening and keep an eye on the trail and the road beyond." He put the bottle on the island and let his smile stretch as she drank. "We've stocked the fridge, cut and stacked wood, something none of my guys had ever done before as far as I know, and put a few cases of some of my father's Barolo in the pantry in case you feel the need to get shitty drunk." He winked at Gin when she shook her head, as though Johnny's good looks were nothing compared to her anger. "It'd be understandable, the shitty drunk you might want to become after the clusterfuck that happened here."

"Yeah," Gin said, pushing away from the island, her bottom lip against the rim of her glass. "I still don't like it." Then the redhead grabbed the bottle and moved out of the kitchen.

Johnny watched her go, tilting his head to keep an eye on her retreating form before he sighed, turning to face us. "Spitfire, sì?"

"She's disappointed," Kit offered, leaning against the island across from my brother. "That attitude has nothing to do with you. I'm sure when she's calmed down she'll warm up to you."

"Thank you, *bella*, but I won't be around long enough for that." He looked at Kiel, then to me before facing Kane. "You want me to answer for that shit with your brother?"

Kane nodded but didn't speak. There was something dangerous in his eyes. Something that reminded me of the warring thoughts I knew ran through Kiel's mind as he stood over Vinnie, debating if he wanted to pummel him with the poker.

"I can respect that," Johnny said, getting comfortable, leaning against the island like Kit. He stretched out his legs and crossed his arms as though he was the most relaxed he'd ever been before. "Right now, though, we've got pressing issues."

"Such as?" Kane asked, shaking his head when Kiel opened his mouth to speak.

Johnny watched the big man, eyes narrowed. "Technically, we're related. Your kid brother, my kid sister, whether either of us likes it. We got ties." Kane didn't react even as Johnny watched him. And after several seconds, my brother continued. "Even if it's distasteful to you, having ties with us can work out."

"How do you figure that?" Kane asked, his jaw working as he grinded his teeth together.

"For starters, we can handle shit when it comes." Johnny gestured around the cabin. "If you've got a mess, it's a good bet I can clean it up for you."

"We clean up our own messes," Kane said. Tension kept his shoulders tight, straight, but neither his stance or his frown did anything to intimidate my brother. Not much did.

"Yeah? Like how after only a couple hours of being here, that asshole found you all?"

"We handled it."

Johnny stepped closer, pushing off the island to stare at Kane. "You got lucky."

When Kane took another step, looking ready to tussle yet again after just having his knuckles taped up, Kiel intervened, holding a hand to his brother's chest.

"That's enough," he said, staring between my brother and his. "Kane, I know you think Johnny owes us for busting me up, but that shit is in the past."

Kane glared at his kid brother, eyebrows shooting up. "You fucking kidding me? He owes you for that..."

"Look around, man," Kiel said, pointing to the clean floors and mended furniture. "You see any of those assholes around here? You see *anything* busted or bloody?" Kane shot a glance around the room but didn't move away from his brother. "Yeah," Kiel continued. "He's paid me back tenfold for what happened. I'm over it." He clapped his brother on the shoulder. "Time for you to get over it too."

It took several long seconds for Kane's expression to change. He didn't speak, didn't react at all as Kiel thanked Johnny for the cleanup and handling the shit we couldn't. Then, when Kit came to his side, Kane reached out a hand, offering it to Johnny.

"Don't much like you, but I appreciate you helping us out."

My brother shook the big man's hand, his features relaxed. "And thank you for keeping my sister safe."

Kane nodded, the movement more like an afterthought when Kit tugged on his arm. "I'm tired, baby. Let's get some sleep." She nodded to Johnny then led Kane through the kitchen to the other side of the cabin.

Kiel waited until the bedroom door shut before he looked back at Johnny, arms crossed as he watched him. "Vinnie and his goons?"

Johnny waited, moving his top teeth over his bottom lip as though he needed time to answer in a way that wouldn't incriminate him or leave us vulnerable. Finally, he shrugged, walking back to the glass door. "Vinnie and his men won't be a problem for anyone anymore."

"Meaning?" Kiel asked, frowning as though he hadn't meant to ask the question.

"Meaning," my brother said, still watching the woods outside that glass door. "Our father handled that business, and no one will ever be bothered by those assholes again." He shot a look over his shoulder, frowning at Kiel. "*Ever*. Again."

Kiel cursed, rubbing his neck. He hated the business my family did. He hated that he'd ended up right where he'd never wanted to be and when he cursed, mumbling something he kept to himself. I touched his wrist, getting him to look down at me.

"First family rule?" I started, relaxing when the tension tightening the muscles in Kiel's face eased. "Don't ever ask questions if you can't handle the answers."

"She's right," Johnny said, finally turning to face us. "And here's an answer I bet you never thought you wanted."

"Which is?" Kiel didn't push my hand away when I tightened my grip around his wrist. Instead, he moved his fingers, locking them with mine.

"*Cazzo,* never thought I'd have to admit this, but since we're here, and since there seems to be nothing in your way anymore..."

"Talk," I said, glaring at my brother. He knitted his eyebrows together, making him look older, like he hadn't gotten much sleep in the past week. I could relate, but that didn't mean I'd let him off the hook.

"Fine," Johnny said, moving to the couch, motioning for Kiel and me to do the same. We did, taking the leather seat across the repaired coffee table. My brother watched us, gaze shifting before he leaned forward, watching his hands, those long fingers of his as he laced them together. "It was my fault." I tilted my head, not understanding, and Johnny nodded, looking nervous when Kiel rested his elbows on his knees like he was ready to pounce.

"Vinnie. I suggested him to Papa for you." My brother ignored the small grunting noise I released then focused on moving his gaze between Kiel and me. "It was stupid, and Papa was so worried you'd be on your own when he..." Johnny waved his hand, as though he couldn't bring himself to mention the inevitable outcome for our father. "Anyway, he had

ideas about seeing you cared for since he knew I'd be...
occupied with the business. And I thought of asking
you what you thought of the situation. But that's when
I walked in on you in Papa's office, looking over the
file the PI sent you." He nodded at Kiel, and I slumped
against the sofa.

"You had me investigated?" Kiel asked, mouth
dropped open as he watched me. I hated that look. I
hated the little hint of betrayal I spotted in his features.

"I wasn't going to interrupt your life if you had
other...ties here." It was a simple explanation, and it
seemed to make Kiel's surprise dim. "Finish," I told
my brother, holding Kiel's hand when he rested it on
my thigh.

"I waited until you left and pulled up your history.
All those articles from the *Seattle Times* that Kiel
wrote. The same Kiel you'd promised had stalked you
for six months. Didn't take much effort to pay off the
PI and find out what you had him looking up. I got the
gist, figuring all the bullshit you told us about him—"
he jerked his chin toward Kiel "—was *total* bullshit."
He shook his head, as though still amazed how many
lies I'd told to get Kiel out of my life. Johnny rubbed
the bridge of his nose, looking tired and frustrated,
but that didn't keep him from continuing. "My own
sister, lying to me. Lying to our father. I got mad at
first. Then, when I gave myself time to think about it,
I figured you had your reasons for lying to the cops."

"Stupid damn reasons," Kiel said, wincing when I
elbowed him in the side.

"Stupid or not, I knew she had a reason, and I knew the way she went on, keeping herself off everyone's radar, not seeing anyone, not doing anything but going to work at the museum. And that fund raiser..." Kiel glanced at me, moving his gaze to my face, then away from it in sudden, swift movements. Johnny caught the look, same as I had, and my brother shook his head, his smile lethal. "The fund raiser wasn't her," he offered, stretching an arm along the back of the sofa. "The money? Hell, man, that was me."

"Johnny!" I glared at my brother, feeling my stomach twist. "Do you have any idea the shit you caused?"

He gestured again, looking impatient. "I replaced it," he admitted. "Or don't you remember the bid on the Matisse no one ever claimed? It got paid for, and you kept the piece with an anonymous, 'With my kind regards' note, remember? That was me. The Matisse more than covered the hundred grand I *borrowed*."

My brother laughed as I kept my glare steady, lowering his shoulders as though he didn't see why I was still so irritated.

"Why did you take the money?" Kiel asked, relaxing against the cushions with his arm around my shoulder.

Then Johnny slipped his gaze to me, lowering it just as quickly. "Sammy?" I asked, trying to hold off smiling. When my brother nodded, I laughed, not caring if I insulted him. "I knew you couldn't have paid them off without anyone finding out." The frown Johnny gave me was sharp, his eyes piercing, which only made me laugh harder. "Give it a rest. Kiel knows. I told him. I tell him everything."

Johnny cursed under his breath, something low and accented, but he didn't comment further on my confession. The curl of his top lip relaxed, and in the next second he seemed more interested in his confession than the fact that I'd told Kiel about young Samantha.

"Like I was saying...Vinnie. I'd figured out your lie and guessed about the why. It was clear you still wanted Kiel, and Papa wanted you married. If I got Vinnie mentioned and pushed him in front of Papa, I knew he couldn't resist."

"Johnny..." I said, too surprised to think of anything to say.

"You needed a push to bring your man back to you. That's what I offered." When Kiel pulled his hand away from mine and started rubbing his palms together, a nervous habit he had, my brother rushed to explain more. "It worked out, didn't it? It got him here, and it got—"

"Our friend Dale shot," Kiel said, his expression fierce.

"I didn't know Vinnie was unstable." Johnny held up his hands, a gesture of surrender that didn't last. "Hand to God, I had no idea what a prick he was or that he'd do anything to get you in front of a priest."

"All of this because I wasn't honest?" I asked, cupping my face in my hands.

"All of this because our father loves you. He wants you looked after."

"Still?" I asked, unable to keep the small flicker of hope from my tone. I'd never gone so long without speaking to my father. No matter who he was and what he did, he was still my father. "You mean he *loved* me. Past tense."

"No, not past. Now. Today. Tomorrow." He moved to the edge of the sofa, pressing his thumbs together, a nervous tic he probably didn't realize he had. "When I told him you'd been shot at, that Kiel had protected you and Arturo and got you out of there and to somewhere safe? Ah, *rella*, he was beside himself. I told him everything that night—about you and Kiel and how he'd never been your stalker. About Vinnie and his side piece he liked to keep at the ready, and how the bastard only wanted to be with you because of our business. Papa was beside himself."

When I blinked, failing to keep the burn of tears from clouding my vision completely, Johnny came to me, kneeling to hold my face in his hands. "He wants you to come home." He glanced at Kiel and nodded. "He wants both of you to come home. I've never seen him so miserable." My brother kissed my forehead, holding me while I cried against his chest. "He's so sorry, *rella,* and he wants his *bimba* back."

"Give us some time," Kiel said, resting his palm on my back as my brother stood. Johnny still held my face, tipping my chin with his knuckle before he nodded, an unspoken answer to Kiel.

"It's been a rough few days," Johnny said, stepping back. He'd gotten a little teary as he held me—I spotted the redness in the whites of his eyes and the dampness on his face. But like the macho guy he thought he was, Johnny wiped a hand over his face and cleared his throat, pretending there hadn't been a small break in his in-control composure.

"Papa will understand. You stay here." He waved around the cabin. "It's a good spot to be alone with the one..." Another motion, this one between Kiel and me, and Johnny's voice trailed off.

He was strong. He was controlled, and there had been only one time I'd ever seen my brother lose himself—and that control—completely. The thought surprised me more than it should have, and despite the ache I felt when I thought of facing my father, despite the violence that had been at the center of our world the past few days, I wondered if Johnny would ever have that loss of control again. Kiel made me crazy. He turned me on. He made it so I couldn't breathe, couldn't *be* unless he was near me. Had Johnny felt that way before? Would he ever have that?

Without thinking, I took my brother's hand, holding his fingers tightly as I watched his face. "Papa will be...gone soon." His mouth tightened, but he didn't try to argue with me. "And I have Kiel, and we'll make a life together. But you, *cucciolo*, you'll have the business. You'll have *only* the business."

It took a minute for Johnny to understand my meaning. In that time, he watched me, frown hardening as though he wasn't sure how to react. Johnny shifted his gaze between Kiel and me, then he relaxed the tension from his face. "Cara, don't worry about me. I have...means. I have company."

"The girls you and your friends pass around don't count." I slipped my fingers between his, hoping he knew that I only wanted him to be happy. Like I was. Like I *finally* was after all this time. "Don't you want to love someone?"

Johnny's attention went straight to Kiel, who must have seen something in my brother's expression that told him this wasn't something he wanted to discuss. Kiel kissed my forehead then went into the kitchen, busying himself with a beer from the fridge.

"Cara, there isn't space for any of that." Johnny sat next to me, still holding my hand, but I got the feeling he did that to appease me.

I expected him to tell me this wasn't my business. Maybe he wanted to lecture me about keeping both of us safe. I didn't care about any of that just then. I wanted my question answered. "Why won't you tell me?"

"Does it matter?" Johnny lowered his voice, but he didn't seem worried about Kiel in the kitchen behind us. For a moment, it was just me and my big brother talking about big, complicated things I wasn't sure we'd ever quite figure out.

"It matters to me, *amore*. I want you to have what I have." He snorted out a laugh, and I pushed his shoulder. "What I have now. Not what I had to go through to get it, but what we have now."

Johnny watched me, eyes squinting, gaze staring straight, unblinking on my face before he exhaled, rubbing the bridge of his nose. "I might have had that once. But I was stupid and young, and...I messed it up."

"Sammy?" I asked, taking the way my brother's jaw clenched as answer enough. "She's not a nun?" He shook his head but stayed silent. "You know where she is?"

"Doesn't matter," he admitted, rising from the sofa.

"Why not?"

Johnny grabbed his phone, pretending to be interested in whatever caught his attention. I didn't care if he didn't want to talk about Sammy. There was something in his eyes when her name came up. Something that made him look both younger and ancient all at the same time.

"Johnny, why doesn't it..."

He grunted, the noise silencing me before he shoved his phone in his pocket. "Because, *rella*. She was never the same after...everything. She never will be again, and that's my fault."

Funny thing was, Johnny hadn't been the same either. I wondered if he ever would be again.

Chapter Eighteen
Cara

As it turned out, three days was a long, *long* time to be around strangers. Kane and Kiel kept busy around the cabin, working on busted fencing, bossing Johnny's men around to help fetch more wood or clear away fallen limbs around the property. They seemed to find things to do, but then, neither man was the type to sit around and be idle. If Kane was anything like his brother, I suspected the same was true for nakedness. There was nothing remotely idle about Kiel, *especially* during naked time.

The days with us—Kit, Gin, and me was a little bumpier. There hadn't ever been much time for friends of my own growing up. It was a hazard of the family I'd been born into. I was the one of only two females among all our cousins, so there wasn't much in the way of female companionship to be found for me. Especially since Antonia thought it would be okay to try to fuck Kiel in the airport. It was odd being relegated to the company of strangers, especially strange women. Kit was crazy about Kane. It was mutual, and I liked her a lot. I'd even started to like Gin before Dale's fuck-up at the hospital. But they were both still strangers.

Gin's attitude had only gotten grouchier, her mood sullen, and there didn't seem to be enough wine in the world to tamp down her anger. Despite Kane's explanation about anesthesia and its side effects, or his belief that Dale harbored some bone-deep longing for Gin, the woman's attitude didn't change.

And it was starting to piss me off.

Kane and Kiel sat around the kitchen table playing cards while Kit joined me and a half-drunk Gin on the balcony, enjoying the blazing warmth of the firepit. This was the last attempt I'd make to get Gin out of her funk. Any more of it and I might have to go a little Carelli on her ass.

"Here," Kit offered, rolling her eyes when Gin refused the chocolate cupcake she offered.

"Give me one," I told her, taking the thing in two hands. The icing was thick, sweet, and creamy, and I made a low, groaning sound when I bit into it. "Jesus, Kit, these are good." I glanced at Gin, offering the cupcake to her. "You're missing out. So fucking good."

"I'm not hungry," she said, leaning back against her chair with her sock feet on the firepit railing.

"Thirsty, though, right?" The question came out before I could stop myself.

"What is that supposed to mean?" She sat up straighter, holding the glass against her chest. When Kit whispered something to her, the redhead shook her head, quieting her friend. "No, I wanna know what that little question is supposed to mean."

The cupcake crumbled a little when I set it on the armrest, and I licked my lips, debating the wisdom of telling this woman how things were or telling her what she wanted to hear. Neither option would have a good outcome, but maybe I could do something to shake her out of her mood.

"Cara," Kit warned, her voice on the edge of worry, but I shook my head, inhaling as I curled my arms over my chest. From my seat, I spotted Kiel smiling, laughing at something his brother said, and I felt something deep inside me hum, warming my entire body.

Gin hadn't relaxed or sat back again, and Kit still shifted her gaze between the two of us as if she was worried what I'd say or do if Gin's drunken insults got out of hand. The redhead was beautiful, athletic, and I'd have to be a blind idiot not to notice how it was between her and Dale. They wanted each other, but something held them back.

Kiel laughed again, flipping the bird at his brother. He stared right at me, offering me a wink as he downed the rest of his beer. I felt sorry for anyone who wasn't me. That man loved me, and I'd given him nothing but hell. He loved me despite all the stress and trouble being with me brought him.

Gin had no idea how to play her cards. I was about to school her.

"Okay," I started, resting my hands over my stomach as I shifted my attention to Gin. She wore an expression that was defensive and defiant, and I'd only spoken one word. She wasn't ready for what I had to say, but I said it anyway. "You and Dale, this whole thing. It's as bad as I think, right?"

"No," she said, a little too quickly. "Don't make assumptions." Gin glared at Kit when the woman started laughing. "What?"

"Oh my God, it's the worst thing ever, watching the two of you." She stared at me, flippantly moving her hand. "Before...the hospital, on set, every day...they dote on each other, just stand around working elbow to elbow and grab coffee for each other. They're each other's shadows. It's actually funny. But let anyone other than the pair of them flirt or engage or try to disrupt their little box and, my God, the fireworks."

"So, they're how you and Kane were?" I asked, remembering the low-down Kiel had given me on the trek up the mountain.

"Yes," Kit said, smiling. "But to the nth degree."

"You're exaggerating," Gin snapped, scrubbing her face. She didn't react when Kit laughed, and I got what this was. Deflection. Gin was still so angry. Kit was using this little chat to interject some humor. Gin had been too intense, too pissed off since the Trudy incident.

"I'm not," Kit supplied, stretching out her long legs to rest her feet next to Gin's on the pit. "I honestly don't know what the problem is."

"Is Dale into her?" I asked, knowing he was but wanting to see Gin's reaction to the question. She sighed, lowering her forehead to her knees.

"Very," Kit said.

"He's not," Gin interrupted, groaning as she sat up and looked between us. "Before...when things were normal," she sighed, and her mouth hardened. I suspected she was trying to fight past the effects of the wine and her rage to remember how things had been between them before the shooting. "He's just a little closed off... That...bitch Trudy did him so wrong."

"They all have bitches in their pasts," I told her, head shaking at Gin's defeated tone. "Is he marble or putty?"

"What?" both women asked, unblinking as they watched me.

"Marble or putty. That's the type of men we're left with. As women, it's a struggle, most times, to find the perfect man. Let's be honest, they don't exist. And so, we're left with marble men and putty men. Depending on what you want, you have to decide which ones you're willing to tolerate." When neither of them spoke, I continued, shrugging because I figured it was self-explanatory. It had been for me when my *Nonna* Maria explained it to me as a young woman fresh out of high school.

I sat up, crossing my legs and leaned one elbow on my knee, gaze shifting between Gin and Kit. "Marble men are obstinate. They require that you work and fret and work even more to chip away the layers. It could take years. It could take you a lifetime, and even after all the drama you've endured chipping away at that marble, you might be left with something beautiful and unique, but you've spent so much of your time whittling away the layers that you don't appreciate the art you've made once you're done. Marble is hard. It's difficult to mold to what you want."

Gin sat up, frowning at me like she wasn't sure where I was heading. Kit seemed to get the analogy, offering a small half smile as I continued.

"Putty, though, is flexible. Putty is easy to mold. It bends and stretches with little effort. It adjusts to your will, and sometimes, if you lay it flat enough, it takes on the shape you want. It doesn't take much effort with putty, and sometimes that's best because you get what you want, and you'll go on getting what you want for as long as you're willing to mold it to your liking. So, you have to decide: do you want this beautiful, obstinate thing that will require a lifetime of work to get to what you want it to be. Or, do you want something that's soft and malleable and yours with careful attention."

Gin tilted her head, watching me, frown deepening as though something had just occurred to her. "I...I don't think Dale is either of those things."

"He's marble," I told her, shaking my head when she started to argue. "You've tried chipping away at that hard stone. It's easy enough to tell. You're with him, around him, there like no one else, I bet, and he still hasn't made a move. Even before that bitch ex of his showed up. There might have been moments, but no moves made, right?" She nodded, slumping back in her chair before she polished off the rest of her wine. "Uh-huh, that's marble." When the muscles around her mouth tightened, I leaned forward, hoping my smile looked more genuine than it felt. "Marble doesn't always stay marble. Sometimes it weakens. Sometimes it will soften with enough attention. Especially," I said, smiling at how focused Gin seemed, watching me, "when they fuck up. Dale did something stupid. He has to know about it."

"He's been blowing up my cell," Gin admitted, glass against her mouth.

"Hmm...mark my words. That asshole is turning to putty."

"Kane's putty," Kit said, sounding proud, and I nodded, agreeing. Then she sat up, eyes shifting into a squint. "What's Kiel?"

"Oh," I said, letting the smile I held widen. This time when it stretched across my mouth, I meant it. "There's no bending Kiel. That mold was broken years ago."

Gin's anger had ebbed. She didn't look happy exactly, but some of the venom in her expression shifted. She stared at the flames, and I thought maybe she'd start to let some of her rage leave her. Dale had done something stupid, but I suspected it wasn't the only time. Hell, if Kiel was right, Dale had dangled possibilities at Gin for years.

Shit or get off the pot, Kane had said to Dale, but he wasn't the only one who needed that lecture.

"Maybe you should…"

Oh shit, I thought, sitting up when Kiel and Kane stood, their attention behind them at the front entrance. Three of Johnny's men ushered Dale inside. The SEAL waved off their help, clapping Kane on the shoulder as he came into the house. Kit caught my nod toward the new arrival, and we shared a look, glancing from the kitchen to Gin, who hadn't noticed the change in our number. Kit stood, grabbing Gin's glass before her friend could stop her.

"I'll get another bottle," she offered and was off the balcony and in the house before Gin could argue.

"You okay?" I asked her, shifting my gaze from the redhead to the kitchen. Kit greeted Dale, gesturing to the bar, but she kept glancing at me. I wasn't sure if she thought I could deflect Gin's anger or maybe distract her, but Kit kept giving me looks, desperate, stupid looks I couldn't decipher.

"Fine," Gin said, and there was less bite in her tone. "This is all just such a mess."

Dale had spotted Gin through the door, and he shook his head when Kane spoke to him, his focus on the balcony and the redhead who still hadn't noticed his arrival.

"Love usually is," I told her, standing when Dale tried to hide the wince he made, opening the door. His expression was calm but firm, and if the man was worried, he didn't give it away. He looked down at Gin, mouth drawn into a line, eyes narrowed so that his bottom lids curved. He wanted to say something, wanted her to listen, that much I read on his expression. But he didn't seem able to do much more than take in her profile, absorbing her sharp features.

When he went on watching, masking whatever he felt behind the hard set of his body and the tight muscles moving his jaw and neck, I intervened, unable to stand the quiet for too long.

"Gin?" I said, watching Dale.

She only lifted her eyebrows, a silent acknowledgment, and when I didn't continue, she glanced up at me, frowning when I nodded toward the door.

"Gingerbread," Dale said, his voice so deep with a gravel that hadn't been there before the shooting. His features were tense, though he let a soft smile twitch one corner of his mouth. It was a welcoming expression, something any woman with a pulse would fall for.

Dale might have a redneck's name, he might be a rough-around-the-edges SEAL, but he was still damn fine. I was married, not dead, and I had noticed the abundance of gorgeous men in the cabin more than once. Kane was almost as beautiful as Kiel, though I was partial. There was something about their beautiful dark skin and wide, tempting frames. But Dale was all muscle and lines, a gruff, disciplined man who never seemed too far from the edge of violence. He was always at the ready, always eager to defend, that much I'd made of him in the short time we'd been at the cabin. Now, though, as he waited for Gin to respond, that big badass looked a little lost.

The redhead stood, pushing the chair away from her. The only sound I noticed was the crackle from the log burning in the pit and the quickening breath that came out of Gin's nose as she watched Dale. He stepped onto the balcony, and I moved around him, leaving them to it as I went to Kiel's side inside the cabin.

We shouldn't have watched. It wasn't our business. I didn't have anything invested in either of them, but Kane loved Dale and Kit loved Gin and Kiel loved them all. They'd be in my circle from now on, no matter where we ended up. Dale stepped closer, jaw working as he stretched a hand toward her, and we couldn't look away. It was some pantomimed, silent display, those two on the balcony, and it was too consuming to ignore.

"Touch him," Kit whispered, seeming to will her friend to meet Dale halfway. And from the look on Gin's face, I thought she might do just that. Next to Kit, Kane held a warming bottle of beer, and both he and Kiel watched their friend, silently, likely as nervous as we were for what would come next.

Then Dale said something, forcing a laugh, but it wasn't anything the redhead seemed to find funny. Instead of taking his hand, Gin crossed her arms, her face pinched as she shook her head and pulled back the glass door.

She was through the living room and to the back of the house before Dale made it inside. He was a large man, well over six-two, dwarfed only a bit by Kane when Dale stood by my brother-in-law. Despite his hard exterior, just then, Dale looked weakened, maybe from the gunshot, maybe from how surely Gin had dismissed him. It took strength to take that kind of rejection, but if he was hurt, physically or otherwise, Dale still stood tall and set his features like he was about to do battle.

"Tell me," he said, looking down the hall to where Gin had disappeared. My brother had done that, but the expression on Dale's face wasn't amused like Johnny's had been. He was determined. Those two words seemed like a request for information, logistics and details he'd need before he began his mission.

Kit released a sigh, patting him on his shoulder, and it was only then that Dale looked away from the hallway. "Oh, honey," she started, all the humor vacant from her tone. "It's as bad as you think it is."

Dale grunted, a low, primal sound that sounded angry and desperate. "Well, then..." He grabbed the beer from Kane's hand, downing it in one swallow. "I best figure out how to unfuck this."

Chapter Nineteen
Cara

The plane, minus a loose-lipped flight attendant, seemed so much smaller to me on the way back to New York than it had when we'd left the city. But then, that could have been from tiredness. Dale had not let things lie with Gin. The gruff, quiet man, it turned out, had a mouth on him when he was angry or desperate or ridiculously sorry. A mouth that kept us awake wincing and tsking all night. From what we heard in the shouting echoes, Gin didn't care about anything Dale had to say. By the time we'd packed and notified the pilots Kiel and I were heading to the airport, Gin had left, and Dale was passed out on the sofa, drunk on pain meds or beer or plain heartache and regret.

The return trip was welcome, and Kiel and I enjoyed it. Even when things got a little bumpy somewhere over Michigan and the turbulence made me feel sick. We'd landed, picked up by a fully recovered Arturo, who'd greeted Kiel with a handshake of thanks and many heavily accented refrains of *"grazie mille"* and *"molte grazie,"* for saving him during the shootout and me with a kiss on each cheek and a warm, grateful smile, I guessed, for having such good taste in men.

Arturo filled me in on the museum and all the guests he'd had while he was in the hospital, while Kiel frowned, staring out the window like he was on his way to his own funeral.

"Relax," I told him, holding his hand. The gesture served its purpose. Kiel turned away from the window, slipping his arm over my shoulder.

"I'm fine. I just..." He closed his eyes, grunting when we pulled up my father's long, landscaped drive. "I don't like drama."

I laughed, unable to keep myself under control. "Oh, *bello*, then you married the wrong damn woman."

He didn't relax, not when Arturo opened the doors, or when Dante and Giovanni greeted us with professional half smiles and nods as we walked inside. Kiel, in fact, didn't relax remotely as we moved down that long, tiled hallway and came into the parlor where my father sat in a wheelchair, right in front of the large wall of windows that looked out onto the lush garden.

If possible, my father looked ten years older than when I'd last seen him. He seemed so small to me now, when all my life he'd been this giant of a man, always leading, guiding, never backing down from anyone. It wasn't often that my papa was cowed by anything. As Kiel and I walked into the parlor of his mansion, the worry that moved across his face and the wrinkles that dented deep into his skin seemed to vanish. He met my gaze, his eyebrows lifting as though he'd just spotted something he'd misplaced and prayed would be returned. That seemed as close to the truth as possible. In his eyes, I had been lost. I'd almost been lost forever.

"*Vita mia,*" he said, his voice lifted in a tone of utter disbelief. "My *bambina.*" Papa raised his arms, and I ran to him, slipping to my knees, cheek against his chest as he held me. "Ah, my *bella amore.*"

"Papa..." There was a little disbelief in my tone too, but I didn't care.

My father had blood on his hands. I guess I did too now. So did Kiel. But he had been threatened, and by association, so had I. One word from me might have saved those lost by my father's command. Vinnie might still be here if I'd just toed the line and done what Papa wanted.

Kiel moved to the side of the chair, his expression soft but wary, and when he met my gaze, offering me a wink that did something funny to my stomach, I realized I wouldn't have changed anything about how we ended up here. He was mine, and I was his. Forever. There was no more threat. There was no more worry for us but how to navigate my father's life and the family we wanted together. Kiel wouldn't be part of the family business. Neither would I.

"Hush now," my father said, pushing me back. "Let me see you. It's been too long." He returned the smile I gave him. I relished the feel of his palm against my cheek. It hadn't been all that long, actually, but to my father, even a day was too long. He went on looking at me, smile wide and brilliant, and though he looked weak and older, he was still handsome, still elegant. One quick glance at Kiel standing next to us and some of the withering traces of illness left his face.

"Kaino," he said. Papa didn't smile at Kiel exactly, but he did stretch his arm, offering him a shake. Kiel took it, bending down a bit to let my father grip him in both his frail hands. "I owe you my apologies," Papa began, shaking his head as he rolled his eyes at me, a small admonishment he didn't mean. "And my gratitude." Kiel nodded, beginning to pull away, but he paused when Papa pulled him forward, refusing to release him. "My daughter, she's my world, *sì*?"

"And mine," Kiel replied, his features firm, sincere. He didn't try to get away from my father again, and he let the old man have his say.

"*Bene,*" Papa said, reaching up to pat Kiel's face. "That is good to hear." He released Kiel and rested back against his chair, hands folding over his lap. "Now, first you must see Father Michaels," he said, nodding at me.

"Why?"

Papa shook his head, tongue clicking as though I'd asked a pointless question. "So we can plan the wedding. But first, I want to ask you, Kiel," he said, his attention turning to my husband. "My son says you are a writer."

"Journalist. Yes."

"Why do we need a wedding?" I interrupted, earning a glare from Papa. I hadn't gotten one of those since I'd snuck out at seventeen to go parking with Alfonse DeAngelo the night of his graduation.

"You will be married in a church, *bella*. In front of a priest and God and the Blessed Mother," my father explained, motioning for me to hush when I opened my mouth again. Papa disregarded me in favor of looking Kiel over as though he needed to get the make of him. "Are you a good writer?"

Kiel shrugged but didn't deny it. "I am."

"*Molto bene*. Come," he said, motioning to the chair next to his. And then, as though he hadn't missed me, as though he had never been disappointed in me for my defiance or worried over my being attacked, my father moved forward, ready to tackle the next item on the unseen list he kept in his head. "We'll discuss a project I have. A book, *sì*? About my life."

"Papa," I fussed, wondering why he'd be so willing to expose himself and his friends for something as trivial as a book, or why he seemed so eager to forget I was standing next to him, uninformed about what he planned.

But my father waved me off, as if my worry was pointless. "An anonymous book, *sì?*"

For the next hour, my father ignored me, drawing Kiel into a lengthy discussion about exclusive, firsthand accounts of criminal masterminds, and how he was old and wanted to retire. He wanted grandchildren and to keep them safe. He wanted Kiel to provide for his *bambina*.

A half hour later and Kiel was all in, excited about what could be. And I realized, with very little effort, my husband had become the one thing he swore he'd never want: a member of the Carelli family.

Chapter Twenty

Kiel

One month later...

"You shouldn't be in here," Cara said, covering her body with the sheet like I hadn't seen, tasted, and touched every inch of her skin already.

I walked toward her, laughing as I stripped off my clothes, fumbling with my jeans as they tangled around my feet. "Come on, baby, don't be like that."

Cara shifted her gaze, eyes narrowing as I finally got my pants off and threw them in the air. "Are you drunk?"

"I never get drunk," I said. My expression was sincere, poker-faced, though I knew that promise was the biggest load of garbage ever. I hadn't planned on getting shit-faced tonight, but Johnny mumbled some nonsense about bachelor parties and welcoming me into the family. Kane told me to stop being a tight ass, pushing the shots in front of me and replacing them as quick as he could. "I'm buzzed."

She crossed her arms over her chest, tightening her grip on the sheet, but her eyes skated down my body and landed on my hard cock. "It's the night before the wedding. You're not supposed to see me."

I yanked at the sheet, but she moved, keeping her naked flesh on lockdown. "We're already married," I reminded her and tugged harder at the fabric, needing to bury myself so deep in Cara that everything else fell away.

She covered her breasts with her arm and sat up a little straighter. "But this time, it'll be before God."

I resisted the urge to roll my eyes because I was horny and damn sure didn't want to have another argument about the lavish, unnecessarily big Italian wedding I'd been roped into. All that mattered was that we were making the entire marriage official for her family, even if they were going over the top. Her father insisted, his one wish before he died. That was how he played the entire thing, using guilt to get his way.

"Baby, you wanna see God tonight?" I quirked an eyebrow as I wrapped my fingers around her tiny ankle from the foot of the bed. "'Cause I can make that shit happen."

"Kiel." There was no amusement on her face as she spoke, but her eyes never left my dick. "Tomorrow."

I thrust my hips out, moving my stiff cock in the air, swaying back and forth, giving her a dick dance. "This ain't waiting until tomorrow, honey."

Cara dissolved into a fit of laughter, and I used the moment to give her ankle a quick pull, bringing her down to the edge of the bed. She screamed as her body moved, but she didn't put up much of a fight. A little tugging and Cara was face-to-face with the one part of me she always claimed to like best.

"Oh, hey there," she said, staring at my cock as I continued to move it.

Gotta admit, I was shameless as hell, but I didn't give a fuck. I wanted my wife, and I'd use any stupid tactic not to have to go back to my room and jack off like a teenager.

"Kiss it," I told her as I tangled my fingers in her dark hair. I didn't know if I'd ever said such dumb shit in all my life, but I rolled with it because she started licking her lips, looking like she wanted to devour my cock. "It'll be our final sin."

Her father was old-school, a little conservative despite the bullshit criminal empire that made him rich. According to Mr. Carelli, we weren't really married because we hadn't said our vows before God. We'd been living in sin in his eyes, and we were going to hell unless we made things right with the church. Wonder what he'd think about the way his son made things right with the church, or at least, the priest who called Johnny a worthless Catholic.

Cara wrapped her hand around the shaft and squeezed. My body quaked uncontrollably like she'd never touched me before, and I held my breath as she leaned forward, waiting for the moment her warm, soft lips closed around me. The air thickened in just those few seconds, the anticipation getting me high, and then Cara peered up at me, her brown eyes blazing, and a small smirk played on her lips. My fingers tightened, urging her forward, but she had other plans.

"You want me to put it in my mouth?" she asked, toying with me like only Cara could. "What are you going to give me?" She raised an eyebrow, stroking my cock faster and torturing me.

"All the orgasms," I told her, completely full of myself because of the drinks, but sex was the one thing I'd always gotten right. I could make Cara fucking come like no one else. It was probably the only reason she never went through with the divorce. I'd ruined her. She knew it. I knew it. And no one else would do her the way I did.

"You know all the right things to say to me, Kiel." She smiled, sticking her tongue out and barely brushing the tip before quickly vanishing as she stared up at me.

I shivered, and my hips lurched forward, begging for more as my cock pushed against her lips. "Baby, stop playing," I mumbled, barely getting the words out from the wicked spinning that was happening in my head.

"Better not fucking pass out on me," she hissed as she tightened her grip, yanking me forward by my cock and wrapping her sweet lips around the tip.

I moved forward, giving her access to every inch of my needy, rock-hard cock. "Wide awake now."

Cara stroked my shaft with her hand in tandem with her mouth working my dick like she was made to do nothing else. Each time taking my dick a little deeper and sending me a lot closer to orgasm. Shit, it felt too good, but I didn't want to come too quick. I wanted to savor the moment, relish the feel of her soft, warm mouth circling and sucking every inch of me. She moaned, sending pleasure through my entire system.

"Fuck," I growled and rocked with her movement, unable to stop myself from enjoying the pleasure only her mouth could deliver. But this wasn't what I'd come here for. I didn't want a quick blow job the night before we said I do. Again. I wanted to be inside my wife. Possess her. Own her. Remind her who she'd always belonged to, so she never forgot. "Enough." I gently pulled back on her hair, easing her down my dick until her lips popped off.

She gazed up at me, her mouth in a perfect O, and blinked. "Why? I was enjoying myself."

Damn it. Cara loved to suck cock, and being a man, I loved how and when she did it.

I slid my hand down her face, cupping her chin in my palm and rubbing the pad of my thumb near her lips. "Bella, I need to be inside you." She smiled as I pushed her backward onto the bed and crawled on top of her. She wiggled, sighing when my heavy weight hit her, and I nipped her lips, growling at the sensation of our skin sliding together. Then I pushed her legs apart with one knee, settling in for what I expected would be a very long and slow fuck. "Tell me you love me," I said as I reached between us, running my fingers through her wetness.

"I-I..." she stuttered, convulsing as my fingers glided over her clit, "love you."

"Tell me you want me." I slid my fingers down, pressing them against her opening, waiting to hear the words I wanted and needed so badly. I knew Cara loved me. I knew she wanted me, but there was something about hearing her moments of vulnerability that made me even harder. She was always so tough and barely let her guard down.

She didn't speak, just stared up at me, gasping for air as I slipped one finger inside, teasing her butt also. Our eyes locked, something passing between us that I could feel in my bones. Words lost in time, left unsaid during the years we'd spent apart. Her fingernails dug into my shoulders as she gripped me so hard, as though I might disappear if she didn't tether herself to me.

"Tell me," I said, teasing her with a second finger.

"I want you." Her voice was breathless and needy when she finally spoke. "I've always wanted you."

I rewarded her admission by curling the two fingers up, stroking her G-spot with each swipe. She gasped, rocking her hips in rhythm with my hand. I knew what I wanted her to say next. Something that wouldn't slide off her tongue quite so easy. "Tell me you need me."

Her grip on my shoulder tightened as she held on to me, her eyes almost glaring.

"Say it," I demanded as I stopped my thrusts, waiting for her to finally admit the thing she hated the most. Needing someone was a weakness in her book, and Cara Kaino never wanted to appear weak, not even to me.

I leaned down, bringing my lips so close to hers as my thumb brushed against the side of her clit. Her pussy convulsed against my stilled fingers, sucking me deeper and silently begging for me to move again. "Kiel," she begged. "Please."

"Just say the words. I promise your world won't end." I smirked against her lips and circled around her clit but never made full contact.

"I..." She lifted her bottom off the bed, pushing her pussy against my hand. But her frustration leveled up when she didn't get close enough, and my beautiful wife grunted when I didn't budge, not giving in to her silent pleas for more. "I need you. Happy now?"

Three words that hit me deep. She'd given me what I wanted, and I didn't hesitate to slide my fingers out and push my cock deep inside her. Our bodies fit together like they were made in one mold. Her soft legs wrapped around my middle, holding my body to hers and my cock deep. "You're mine forever, Cara," I told her, and there was no hesitation in my words. "I own every inch of you."

She nodded, unable to speak as I thrust so deep, I almost lost my own breath. I slipped my hand under her ass, tilting her bottom so I didn't miss an inch of her lushness, and I cradled the back of her head in my other hand, holding her as close as possible. "I love only you," I told her, slowly rocking into her, making sure my stare was still locked right on to hers. "I've always only loved you, Cara."

She licked her lips, fingernails firmly planted, ankles locked. "I own every inch of you too, husband," she said, and there was nothing about that statement that wasn't true. "I want this forever."

"You have me for an eternity," I said, brushing my lips against hers as I moved my hips quickly, rocking us both closer and closer to oblivion.

"It'll never be enough," she whispered.

Epilogue
Kiel

One Year Later

Cara didn't like whales. For someone whose ancestry was rooted in the lush culture of Capri and the beautiful coastal living that city enjoyed, my wife didn't have much love for the water at all. Which made the move back to Seattle a little odd.

"Porca miseria, Kiel, what the hell is in this?" she fussed, her arms full of a box marked JUNK KIEL DOESN'T NEED.

That stung a little. I pulled the box from her arms before she could tear into it. It was stuff that wasn't important, but it was still *my* stuff, and I couldn't let go of it. Most of it was relics from high school, my old class ring and yearbooks, possibly a garter Melissa Dix had worn at junior prom—I'd kept it on my rearview mirror like a real douchebag for six months after I'd finished high school. There were also letters in that box, stacks of them that I'd written to Cara after I'd come back home, after she'd had Johnny throttle me like I'd stolen something and didn't know where I'd put it.

"Why won't you let me see?" she asked, growling when I held the box over her head. The round curve of her stomach peeked out from her oversize shirt, and I forgot all about the box and Melissa Dix and the stupid things I'd written Cara when I was so sick over her and hurt that writing it all down was the only way I got through most days.

Hmm. Maybe I should give Dale a heads-up about writing that shit down. It might get that asshole out of the stupid-shit habit he'd been in since Gin left for Portland.

"It's nothing, Little Goddess. Just stuff that used to mean something to me."

"Oh," she said, stepping back to cross her arms over her ever-growing chest. "So, old girlfriend crap?"

I shrugged, more interested in that belly and the size of her already ample tits. She tried pushing me away from her as I dropped the box and curled my hands around her hips, my mouth already heading for her cleavage. But Cara gave up the fight, making a sweet sound that had my cock twitching. "I like it when you make that sound," I admitted, pulling her onto my lap as I flopped to the floor.

"Stop...don't!" The fussing wasn't real. There was too much laughter, a bit too much moaning in her words, and Cara gave up, letting me kiss her stomach when I pushed her shirt up. "Don't mess with my fat belly."

"I made this belly, Goddess. If I wanna mess with it, I will." She groaned, pushing on my shoulder before she fanned her fingers through my hair. "You're wasting time. Your brother and Kit will be here to help us unpack."

"So?" I said, pushing the shirt up to get at those full breasts.

"So, you don't want them to walk in on us being all *coupley* while we're supposed to be unpacking our new house, do you?"

"Please," I admitted. "Do you know how many times I've showed up at their place and had to listen to repeated and endless moans of 'Oh yeah, baby. Squeeze me, harder!' and worst of all, 'Fuck, Kit, you're so tight.' It's embarrassing."

"Exactly my point," Cara said, shoving me off her as she came to her knees. She grabbed the box I'd thrown to the floor and opened the top, shooting glances my way as though she wanted to make sure there wouldn't be retribution, the hot kind, if she opened it.

"If you must," I told her, leaning back on one elbow.

She took out the ring, tilting her head like it was sweet, seeing that dirty gold ring with the stock figure of a football player and the school crest in the center. Cara slipped the class ring onto her thumb and continued to pilfer through my pointless shit.

"Ah. Old girlfriend?" she asked, twirling the garter on a finger. The elastic band was frayed, and the dark maroon ribbon threaded between the lace had dulled in the sun coming from my windshield and was now bright pink.

"No, junior prom date. She wasn't a girlfriend."

"Then why'd you keep this?"

"Because," I told her, reaching for the nasty thing to take it out of her hand. "Teenage boys think shit that remotely implies you got laid is the coolest shit ever."

"So you didn't fuck her?" She nodded to the forgotten garter I'd tossed near the stack of crumpled newspaper and flattened boxes. "Miss Junior Prom?"

"Oh no, I totally fucked her. My first."

Cara wrinkled her nose, muttering something low and offensive in Italian before she went back through the box, and I said a little prayer, grateful I'd convinced her to move back to Seattle to raise our baby. New York was a fine city, but it wasn't home, and God knew there were too many criminals flitting in and out of her father's home, even through the museum, to keep my mind clear of worry over her and the baby.

I shook away the thought of the life we could have had in New York and just watched her. God, she was beautiful. Her skin glowed, actually glowed, and I wondered if it was supposed to be that way. Did all pregnant women look that luminous? That beautiful? Was it hormones, or was it just sheer happiness that lit them up from the inside?

"What…" She pulled out the stack of letters, frowning, holding them in her lap so she could flip through them. They were labeled with her name but not addressed. "What is this?" she asked, holding up the thickest letter among the stack. "My name is on all of these."

"It is," I said, slipping closer to her. I fingered the corner of one yellowed envelope, then leaned back on my palms, watching my wife as she kept that frown hardened the more she fanned through the envelopes.

"When did you write them?"

It was embarrassing to admit, but there weren't any secrets between us. You didn't fall in love with a mafia princess and get away with keeping secrets. There were things I knew about her family, her father, thanks to the long conversations we'd had working on his anonymous real-crime biography, that would scare the most violent of thugs straight. Cara knew as much as I did. I knew the things she'd sworn she'd never tell a soul. This would be no different.

"When I got back to Seattle." I shrugged, not bothered by her surprise. "If you want to read them, you can. But I gotta warn you, there's a lot of anger and hurt in those letters. I hated you for a long fucking time."

Cara's face fell as she watched me, and the grip she held on the letters loosened the longer she stared, blinking, likely recalling everything we'd said and done and wanted for our lives before she got scared and I got stupid.

"I...I don't think I wanna read about how much you hated me." She closed her eyes, dropping the letters as she rubbed her face. "I'm sorry I..."

"Baby," I said, stopping the apology before she could finish it. "I got shot at for you. I beat some asshole bloody for you, so did my brother and Dale. Hell, I married you twice and have spent hundreds of hours listening to your father talk about the shady shit he's done in his life." I pulled her close, draping one of her muscular legs over my thigh. "Monumental things, remember? Every one is for you."

"Kiel," she whispered, pulling my face close to take my lips. Her mouth was firm, and the seductive graze of her skin on mine made my chest constrict. Cara never failed to seep down inside me and squeeze my heart—in the best possible way. When she pulled back, soft fingers still against my face, my wife exhaled, giving her head a small shake. I didn't know what she thought or what she wanted, but there was something sweet, something determined, glinting in her eyes.

"Monumental," she repeated, running her thumbs over my cheeks. "This is it, isn't it?"

"What?" I asked, holding her hand in place when she tried to move it away.

"Our forever." She motioned around the room and to the small swell of her growing stomach. "You, me, and him. Is this it?"

"Yeah," I told Cara, pulling her close. "This is the forever we're making. It started a long time ago."

"When you came back to me?" she asked, leaning against my chest. She played with the loosening collar of my T-shirt, and her warm breath flirted against my neck.

"No, baby," I said, kissing her forehead. "Forever started the first day I saw you." It had been in her modest office with the chestnut desk. There'd been a small mug of espresso in the center of that desk and nothing else. "You didn't stand when I walked into the room, but you smiled at me, and that was enough."

Cara sat up, watching me, her eyebrows pushed together and a faint line working between her eyes. "Enough for what?"

Head shaking, I brushed back the damp hair from her forehead and spent a few long seconds kissing her lips, never wanting it to end. "You. Me, Goddess," I said, smiling at my beautiful wife for the monumental things we'd done and the greater one we were working toward. "You and me and forever."

Nailed Down

CHELLE BLISS
EDEN BUTLER

Chapter One
Kane

"I am the storm."

The guy only blinked at me, a little boy staring at something he didn't seem able to place. "You're... Wait, what?"

It was a problem that reared its tiny head anytime the producers sent another intern to me. They tended to scare easy or, you know, not scare at all. Couldn't let that shit slide. This was especially the case with the ones who had a dad or granddaddy or, *Christ*, girlfriend's father who knew someone who knew someone in the damn business. Even if we were just a small DIY cable network show, we were still Hollywood-ish. That meant favors. That meant I got landed with punk interns who didn't know a wrench from a garden hoe.

"I asked what you do." The kid closed his mouth, eyebrows up, hidden behind those thick black frames he wore. I didn't need to look him over too closely. I'd figured out his type when he hurried onto the set and darted straight for me before I was able to get half a mug of coffee down my throat. He didn't need my attention, not this damn early. Not looking the way he did—stupid glasses he probably didn't need and a bowtie, a fucking green striped bowtie and suspenders, and it wasn't anywhere near Halloween, God help me.

Hipster bullshit. Hipster bullshit I didn't have time for.

"So, when you say you're the storm..."

Fingers tightening around my mug, I worked my jaw, ignoring the kid as Dale and Gin came onto the set, dropping an armful of cut 1x4s onto the wood subfloor. The sound moved around the wide-open cabin and echoing right against the framing and exposed windows.

"He's the storm," the kid told Dale, a pathetic, forced laugh flicking that waxed mustache of his against his bottom lip. "Can you believe that?"

Dale was Navy. Twelve years. I'd hired him four years back—he didn't have a daddy or buddy in the fancy producer's trailer. The guy was good and got the job because he knew his shit. We'd grabbed a few beers the night after his first day so he could ask questions. I gave all my crew that shot. One time, only one, to ask what they wanted about me. After that, curiosity was off the table.

Dale had gotten the measure of me after three pints of Guinness. But the hipster intern? Yeah. That wasn't going to happen.

"He is the fucking storm." Dale said that with a finality that made the intern frown. Had the kid staring between me, nursing my cooling dark roast, and Dale, glaring down at the kid, stare weaving over the damn bowtie, the thick, curled mustache before he flared his nostrils, disgusted.

"The storm, kid. That's Kane. He's a hurricane when we're on a deadline. He's a tsunami when we fuck up. And if you do that too much, he's a motherfucking typhoon. You either handle your shit or prepare for the storm."

Maybe it was Dale's voice—that "Don't. Just don't." vibe every SEAL threw off no matter how long they'd been out of the service, but that sage bullshit wisdom worked. The kid jumped up, hardly managed to bother with a nod at me before he followed after Dale, picking up his drill, tugging on a tool belt that dirtied his stupid hipster skinny jeans.

I downed the rest of my coffee, holding back a laugh when the kid threw a glance over at me then jerked his attention away as I pointed to myself, mouthed "the fucking storm," and shot him the bird.

Damn straight. New season, the whole of which we'd spend a few miles from the entrance to Mount Rainier National Park renovating a huge log cabin, and a brand-new intern to torture. Hell, it was stupid, but I didn't party like I used to. Had to find some kind of fun where I could.

I gave the kid a day, maybe two. Once he realized this gig wasn't grabbing coffee for the producers or standing in for the grips or camera people, once he realized there was a hell of a lot of work to do, then he'd get bored or scared and head out with his tail between his legs. Or suspenders. Or custom Converse.

Dale barked orders at the kid as Gin fought with Mario, the floor contractor. The general bustle of bullshit that came along with the setup the crew did for shooting got louder, the noise annoying, gearing up to piss me right off. And then, somewhere about an hour into our day, all that shit went quiet. It was a silence I was familiar with; had heard it years before when kids at school back in Seattle saw me for the first time after my old man took a dirt nap. Funny thing about death. People are sorry for you, but they feel compelled to ignore you. Someone you love dies, and the world acts like you were the one who bit it. They don't have a damn clue what to say. They only know they can't mention death or dying or how much it sucks. So, in general, you get the silent treatment because, bottom line, people are self-centered, graceless assholes. Anyway, that was the thought I had, the familiar silent sting I recognized when all the noise on the set went still.

It meant Kit was back.

The kid was the only one still yammering on. Hands around an extension cord, Hipster was boring

Gin stupid about some shit I didn't care enough to listen to. I only knew she was listening to him because she jabbed him in the rib as I walked through the set, bypassing gawking, awkward folk watching as Bill, our producer, spoke to Kit like she was a kid, not the talented badass host of our show. He was doing the bumbling, clueless shit. A glance around the set, the stares she got as she walked into the cabin, and I realized everyone did the same—stared and gaped and looked like assholes in the process.

She kept her dark gaze on the top of the cup of coffee she held, listening to Bill as he patted her shoulder, as he made pointless attempts to distract her from the suck she'd landed in.

"So, you...um...I..." Bill spoke in monosyllables, some freakish jackass language he clearly didn't have a handle on. "What I mean is..."

"Look," Kit said, waving off his muttering stupidity with a shake of her head. "I get that this is weird, and you don't know what to say, but I'm okay."

"You really don't have to be back yet, sweetheart." It was hard not to laugh at the glare on Kit's face. She thought Bill was some reject from the seventies no one had clued in to the notion that it was definitely not okay to pinch a woman's ass or call a professional "sugar" or "sweetheart." I mean, shit. He was from California. Not Georgia. There was zero excuse for the sweet talk.

"I'm fine," she mumbled, hid those two words behind a long drink from her Styrofoam cup, and kept her gaze downcast, stifling the glare I knew was there.

"Babe, I know it's been hard." Bill stood a little closer than I liked, and I thought about breaking it up, telling him to go fuck himself, but I knew Kit wouldn't appreciate the big brother shit. She wasn't a princess. She was a fucking general. She could cover her own ass.

"I know you and your cousin were close." Bill put that flabby arm around her, and Kit straightened her shoulders, taking a step to the right to slip out of his reach. "Losing someone you're close to, well, I can imagine."

"Can you?" She didn't wear a lick of makeup. The chicks in the back trailer with all the girl shit hadn't gotten to her yet, and still Kit looked like something out of a Zeffirelli film; young, vibrant, skin like silk, eyes large and dark. Her face was heart-shaped, cheekbones pronounced, russet-colored eyes round with large lids. I loved her big eyes, how dark they were, how she kept everything she thought right behind them, never letting anyone see what went on in her head. She was beautiful, shaped with tempting curves and an athletic build, but her legs were long, and her ass was plump and spectacular. She looked like she belonged on the side of a B-52 bomber, inspiring fighting men to keep at it, not on some small DIY program that only drunks coming in from partying and newborn parents saw at four a.m.

"If you need anything," Bill tried again, but Kit cut him off, directing a wide, toothy smile at him that held more cyanide than sweetness behind it.

"Thank you, Bill. Really. And thank you for the flowers. They were nice." Then Kit grabbed his hand, dropping it from her shoulder. "But the only thing I want to do is get to work."

The quiet kept on, with the crew puttering with busywork shit that didn't need handling, all in weak attempts to watch Kit and Bill. It pissed me off, especially when those nosy assholes kept at their staring even when I stepped into the center of the room.

To my left, Kit was squaring off at Bill, challenging him with a glare to get any closer to her. She might not need me to do the big brother bullshit, but the crew did need reminding there was work to be done.

"Enough of this!" I shouted, not bothering to keep the bite out of my tone. "Get back to work." That staring moved from Kit and lingered on me, but only until I moved up an eyebrow and shouted, "Now!"

They scattered like a bunch of ants whose hill had been kicked by a mean fourth grader, but at least they got moving. Kit came at me a half a second later, standing at my side while she looked over the cabin. Two slow sips from her cup and one swipe of her gaze up to the roof and she finally spoke.

"You get the new header?"

I watched right along with her, pushing back the slow whiff of something sweet I caught coming from her hair. "Be here on Thursday. First thing in the morning." We stood there for several long seconds just watching the room, taking in the exposed beams and the looping wire curling through the walls. I could almost hear the gears in her head shifting, like she had something to say but didn't need me to fish it out of her.

When she went on drinking her coffee, I answered the questions she didn't voice but knew she had. "That shop in Shelton had your stove." She looked up at me then, and I thought I could make out a slow-working grin moving the side of her mouth. The woman liked her appliances. The older, the better. "It's a 1930 Aga. Black with copper fixtures. Fully restored."

Kit turned then, full smile now, and I shifted a glance down at her, head shaking at the flash of something ridiculous and fucking sweet in her eyes. "Stupid expensive?"

"Obscene."

That smile was lethal now, and if she'd been a less classy chick, I'd have sworn she was about to shimmy. Can't say I'd hate seeing that. "And Bill knows how much it was and still let you buy it?"

I shrugged, then nodded a thanks when Gin paused near us, close enough to hand over a refill on my coffee. She turned to Dale, offering him the same, and I cocked an eyebrow at the look he gave her. "I was convincing."

"Ha. You were intimidating," Kit said, nudging me with an elbow. "Thanks. That makes me happy."

"It's why I'm here." I hid the smug grin I wore behind my coffee, telling myself it wasn't stupid to feel like a chump for making the woman happy. I liked when she was happy. Mainly I liked being the man to do the job, but that shit came from somewhere I didn't bother thinking about. No need to imagine things when I knew the truth: Kit Carlyle was my friend, but fuck, did I want to be a helluva lot more than that.

"I don't know what I'd do without you," she admitted, and some stupid, ridiculous thing in my gut went all wobbly. But if Kit noticed the break in my composure—and the quick blink of my eyes and a long, slow sip from my mug to keep me from saying something stupid—she didn't mention it. Instead, she looked around the cabin, nodding a greeting to Gin when she smiled as she moved past us before I felt another nudge on my arm. "I need to run something by you."

"Such as?" But she went all quiet again, out of character when Kit wanted something, enough that I turned to watch her, eyebrows shooting up when she cast a look all around, looking damn guilty or stupid nervous. I couldn't tell which. "Something up?"

"Well, it's just that I need..."

"Hey, *Mr. Storm*..." The intern started laughing at himself before Kit stepped back, clearing her throat as though she didn't want this little punk to know she was about to say something only for my ears. That just pissed me off.

"You see me standing here speaking to someone?" I asked the kid, tilting my head to glare at him. He nodded, then looked to Kit as though she might tell him it was okay to interrupt us. But the woman's attention was on her phone when she took it out as a distraction. I snapped my fingers, bringing the kid's attention back to me. "Go. Away."

"Look, Kane..." But Hipster didn't get a chance to bug me any further. Dale approached, taking the kid's shoulder to turn him, then gave the boy a gentle shove to lead him back toward a stack of 1x4s. The saws started up after that, and I nodded toward the door, getting Kit to follow me out of the cabin and down the driveway until we were at my silver F-150. She hopped right in when I opened the door for her, curling her arms over her chest as though she were frozen solid. The woman was always cold, no matter the temperature, and always bitched that I never ran the heat in my truck.

"All right," I said, my head shaking at how she blew on her fingers like we were in the Arctic and not in a small wooded area intersected by Copper Creek. "Jesus." Then I flipped on the heater and moved the vents toward her. "Now. Whatcha got?"

"Oh." Kit went a little shy on me, way out of character, and I forgot about everything else but the small slip of fear that started crowding my head. This woman never shied away from telling me what to do or what she needed and the fact she wouldn't look at me put me on edge.

"Hey," I said, leaning over my steering wheel and moving my head toward her, trying to catch her attention. "What's wrong?"

"Nothing... It's just..." She exhaled and rubbed her eyes. I could make out the frown behind her hands when she scrubbed her face, and for some reason, that bullshit worry grew more intense. Finally, through a long breath, Kit looked at me straight on, licking her lips like I'd seen her do a thousand times. That shit meant trouble. I'd seen it firsthand. That slow, preparing for battle lip lick meant shit was about to get twisted. "Kane," she said, squaring her shoulders, "I need you. I need only you."

Fuck me, I was in trouble.

About Eden Butler

Eden Butler is an editor and writer of Romance, SciFi and Fantasy novels and the nine-time great-granddaughter of an honest-to-God English pirate. This could explain her affinity for rule breaking and rum.

When she's not writing, or wondering about her *possibly* Jack Sparrowesque ancestor, Eden impatiently awaits her Hogwarts letter, writes, reads and spends too much time watching New Orleans Saints football, and dreaming up plots that will likely keep her on deadline until her hair is white and her teeth are missing.

Currently, she is imprisoned under teenage rule alongside her husband in Southeastern Louisiana. Please send help.

WEBSITE – edenbutler.com
TWITTER – twitter.com/EdenButler_
FACEBOOK – www.facebook.com/eden.butler.184
READER GROUP – https://bit.ly/2kzMnsf
GOODREADS – goodreads.com/author/show/7275168.
Eden_Butler

Subscribe to Eden's newsletter http://eepurl.com/VXQXD for giveaways, sneak peeks and various goodies that might just give you a chuckle.

About Chelle Bliss

Chelle Bliss is the *USA Today* bestselling author of the Men of Inked and ALFA Investigation series. She hails from the Midwest but currently lives near the beach even though she hates sand. She's a full-time writer, time-waster extraordinaire, social media addict, coffee fiend, and ex-high school history teacher. She loves spending time with her two cats, alpha boyfriend, and chatting with readers. To learn more about Chelle, please visit her website.

JOIN CHELLE'S NEWSLETTER
➔ chellebliss.com/news
FOLLOW CHELLE ON BOOKBUB
➔ chellebliss.com/bb

Release Text Notifications (US only)
➔ Text **ALPHAS** to **24587**

Want to drop me a line?
authorchellebliss@gmail.com

or visit:
www.chellebliss.com

Acknowledgements

From Eden Butler:

Thank you to Chelle, who is bossy and blunt and freakin brilliant. I love you so much.

Thank you to my Saints & Sinners, my ARC group and beta readers, and to all the blogs and reviewers who have helped to support my stories. You're encouragement is immeasurably appreciated.

Renita McKinney—you're baller as hell and I love you. Curtis is good people too!

Thanks to my friends, my nieces and family who continue to love and support me even when I don't have a couple of hours to visit or drink wine or do the things normal women do because I'm usually on a deadline. Who am I kidding? There's always time for wine.

As always, thanks to my Bints, especially Judy, Amy, Angela, Leighenne, Yaara and Shannon for the beautiful friendship we've shared for the past fifteen years. It means more than I can say.

And to my family, Barbara Blakes, Marie Anderson-Simmons, Kalpana Singh, Sarah Cooper, and Sherry Jackson, and to my girls, Trinity, Chelsey,

Faith and Grace, our Lil Moon Baby Jax and my forever love, Chris, thank you for never failing to lift me up or love me when I don't deserve it and for never failing to make me feel like the luckiest woman alive. I love you all!

From Chelle Bliss:

Thank you to Eden, who puts up with my bullshit like nobody else. You handle my bossiness like a champ and roll with the punches, soaking up everything I say. I'm not always right. HA! There... that's in print forever.

Thank you to my reader group — Chelle Bliss Romance Hangout and the ladies in Bliss Buzz for helping to keep me motivated. To my betas and ARC readers...thank you for always being there for me.

To my readers — Your words of encouragement are appreciated more than you'll ever know. I can't thank you enough for loving my characters. I write for you as well as myself.

To my family — thanks for loving me. To my friends — thanks for loving me.

To Lisa A. Hollett and Julie Deaton, thank you for making my words, which are sometimes a hot mess, and making them readable and grammatically correct. You ladies are my rocks.

I don't know what else to say and I probably forget dozens of people, but that doesn't mean you aren't valuable. Every person in my life is part of my journey and I thank you for always being there for me.

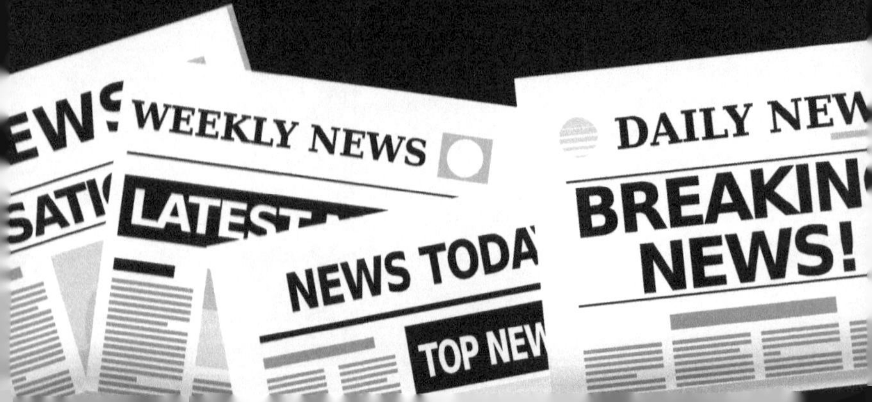
WEEKLY NEWS
LATEST
NEWS TODA
TOP NEW
DAILY NEW
BREAKIN
NEWS!